POINTS
NORTH

POINTS NORTH

STORIES

Howard Frank Mosher

St. Martin's Press

New York

To Phillis

aka

Lake Pontchartrain Templeton

POINTS NORTH. Copyright © 2018 by Howard Frank Mosher. All rights
reserved. Printed in the United States of America. For information,
address St. Martin's Press, 175 Fifth Avenue, New York, NY 10010.

www.stmartins.com

The Library of Congress Cataloging-in-Publication Data
is available upon request.

ISBN 978-1-250-16193-2 (hardcover)
ISBN 978-1-250-16194-9 (ebook)

Our books may be purchased in bulk for promotional, educational,
or business use. Please contact your local bookseller or
the Macmillan Corporate and Premium Sales Department
at 1-800-221-7945, extension 5442, or by email at
MacmillanSpecialMarkets@macmillan.com.

First Edition: January 2018

10   9   8   7   6   5   4   3   2   1

Contents

1

Points North

The Great Earthen Dam at the mouth of the Upper Kingdom River had been obsolete for decades. Originally, the dam had been designed to flood out the hairpin bend in the notch upriver, where the log drives jammed up each spring. Before the dam went in, a small lumberjack or a powder-boy, often Freeman, had been lowered into the notch in a basket to stick a bundle of lighted dynamite into the jam. They'd yank him up fast, with the basket swinging wildly, before the TNT went off and sent the logs flying like so many toothpicks. Freeman had been scared half out of his wits, but overcoming his fear was part of the excitement. There'd been no log drives on the Upper Kingdom now for sixty years. Freeman, the self-appointed dam keeper, was as obsolete as the dam itself, nor would he ever dream of letting his own grandson work as a powder-boy or a jack. He and his grandson were the last two residents of New Canaan, and it wouldn't do to run out the line.

As he'd often told the grandboy, Freeman had seen it all and done it all. Bringing down the log drives with a hundred brawling rivermen in red shirts and spiked boots. Helping build the dam, and the spur rail line from the Common up to Magog, at the head of the lake. During Prohibition Freeman had run booze out of Canada in a battered motor launch. Later he'd worked on the grain freighters coming down the St. Lawrence from the Great Lakes.

"Why did you come back?" the boy asked in an accusing tone.

"Because I was a damn fool, that's why," Freeman said.

This morning Freeman was drawing down the dam. He drew down the dam every fall for no other reason than that his daddy and, before him, his granddaddy had drawn down the dam. Back when the Great Earthen Dam provided power for the Common, there was a point to drawing it down. Freeman's granddaddy and daddy let out the water annually to clear the penstock, clean the turbines, and patch any leaks. The turbines had been pulled out by their blocks and sold for scrap metal years ago. Not long afterward the log drives ended, but if Freeman and the dam were obsolete, they would be obsolete without apology. In the meantime he and the boy supported themselves selling fish in the Common, digging a little ginseng, and guiding downcountry sports.

Just now Freeman was cranking up the gate. He'd inserted his granddaddy's pickpole between two opposite spokes of the bull wheel and was walking around the wheel in a circle, pushing the pole. Nearby the boy fished off the spur line trestle. Watching Freeman walk around the wheel put him in mind of a line from an old number his grandfather played on his granddaddy's violin. *The mule went around with its foot on the ground*. The boy couldn't get the line out of his head. He'd offered to spell Freeman, but the old man wouldn't hear of it. He was as stubborn as the mule in the fiddle tune.

"Your bob is going," Freeman said.

"That's just a little sunnyfish noodling with the minnie," the boy said. "I ain't studying no panfish this morning."

Freeman suspected that the boy was right. A game fish would run with the minnow, then stop to turn the bait in its mouth, then run again. Freeman had trained the boy to strike when the fish stopped the second time. He couldn't fault the grandson when it came to fishing. Most days the boy outfished his granddaddy two fish to one. Lately the sports they guided had preferred to go out on the lake with the boy. He put them over more fish.

The main trouble with the boy was that he reminded Freeman of himself. A year ago Freeman had caught his grandson slipping the fishing knife he'd given him into his lunch bucket. "What do you propose to do with that scaling blade at school?" he'd said.

The boy shot him a defiant look. "What scaling blade?"

Freeman looked at him steadily. Finally the boy said, "I'm going to panic them young'uns that called me a nigger yesterday."

"That won't be necessary," Freeman said. "As of this morning I'm pulling you."

Freeman said this the way he might announce that he was going out to the garden behind the cabins to pull up a turnip. The boy looked at him as if he were speaking Turkish.

"Out of school," Freeman said. "I'm pulling you out of school. How does that suit you?"

"Fine," the grandboy said. "It suits me just fine."

Freeman calculated that the boy was about fourteen. He looked closer to sixteen, which is what Freeman'd told the truant officer the following week.

"That isn't my understanding, Mr. Freeman," the officer said. He looked at the boy, who was staring back at him in an unsettling manner. "How old are you really, son?"

Before the boy could reply Freeman said to him, "Fetch the deer rifle."

"Do you see that goose decoy over yonder by the island?" Freeman said. "Shoot its head off."

The decoy, which Freeman and the boy had set out the evening before to lure in snow geese, was about two hundred yards away. So fast that, as the truant officer reported an hour later to the school principal, he would not have been able to testify in a court of law that he actually saw the boy do it, Freeman's grandson jerked the gun to his shoulder, sighted in the decoy, and pulled the trigger. The bird's head vanished.

"That's how old he is," Freeman said to the truant officer. "Now get on back to town."

This morning, after he finished raising the gate, Freeman would need the boy for cover. An old man with a boy and a couple of fish poles could still go anywhere in the Kingdom unnoticed, not that there was apt to be anyone to notice them where they were headed. Also Freeman wanted to show the boy his heritage. He wanted to show him once and for all who he was and where he came from.

The boy's red-and-white bobber was bouncing. It dived under, popped back up, disappeared again. The line cut through the water, stopped, slanted off toward the middle of the impoundment, stopped once more. The boy struck. A minute later he heaved a smallmouth bass up onto the trestle. "Supper," the boy said. Freeman resumed cranking up the gate.

At one time the boy had belonged to Freeman's ex-daughter. The former daughter had defected to the Common when her mama finally played out from the terrible isolation of living five miles up the lake from the nearest neighbor with, of all people, Freeman. The girl, for her part, had yoked up with trash from the no-count Lord Hollow branch of the Kinneson family. Several years later the fugitive ex-daughter and the ne'er-do-well lit out on the fair circuit to operate a Tilt-A-Whirl. Just before departing they'd deposited the boy, then about six, on the log stoop of Freeman's cabin. A note pinned to his overalls said, "Over to u."

Freeman had been out on the lake fishing for walleyes on the day they saddled him with the grandboy. When he nosed the launch into the wharf in front of the cabin and cut the motor, the boy said in a sharp voice eerily like Freeman's own, "Who are you?" As though the fishing camp and wharf and launch and dam belonged to him and Freeman was the interloper. Although Freeman had never before laid eyes on the boy, he knew immediately who he was from the resemblance to himself. The censorious voice. The pale blue eyes. The reddish glint in his dark hair, which Freeman's granddaddy claimed came down from an overseer in the woodpile.

"I'm your grandfather," Freeman said.

"You and Santy Claus," the boy said. "I don't got no grandfather."

"You do and I'm him and from now on you'll do as I tell you or else," Freeman said.

"We'll see about that," the boy said.

"We will," Freeman said. "In the meantime, what's your name?"

"That's for me to know and you to find out."

Conversing with the boy was like playing a big fish. Sooner or later you had to get him coming your way. After surveying the foundling silently for a few moments, Freeman said, "Do you like to fish?"

"I don't mind," the boy said.

"Get in the boat," Freeman said.

Over the next two hours Freeman let the boy catch a bucketful of yellow perch. He showed his grandson how to fillet them on a cedar plank. After supper the boy stared at him bleakly for a full minute. Then he said, "Name W Kinneson."

"What does it stand for?" Freeman said. "The W?"

"It don't stand for nothing," the boy said. "Just W."

Freeman shook his head. Naming a boy with an initial that stood for nothing was exactly what he'd expect the ex-daughter and the Lord Hollow trash to do. Somewhere he remembered hearing the no-count referred to as Bill. "I imagine it stands for William," Freeman said. "How's about I call you Will?"

"You'll call me W or nothing at all," the boy said.

"I don't intend to call you by some heathenish letter."

"Well, then," the boy said. "I reckon we have us a standoff."

With this the battle between them for ascendancy had begun.

. . .

By sunup the dam gate was nearly wide open. The discharge from the impoundment spewed through the gateway into the lake like water shooting out of a gigantic fire hose.

"I wish it was a schoolhouse full of young'uns like them that called me a nigger that we could drownd out this morning," the boy said. "Wouldn't they squeak, though."

"That puts me in mind of my granddaddy's granddaddy," Freeman said. "Have I told you about him?"

"No more than a hundred times," the boy said. "We can forgo that yarn today if it's all the same."

Forgoing one thing or another if it was all the same was an expression that the boy had picked up from his grandfather.

"It isn't any yarn," Freeman said. "It's true history. My granddaddy's granddaddy, Running Tobe, was a slave in the Dominion of Old Virginy. When he was fifteen, Tobe ran north. They put the dogs on him, sent the slave catchers after him. The dogs and the slave catchers never came back."

Freeman looked at the boy to make sure he understood the significance of the dogs and slave catchers failing to return to Old Virginy. "When he got to the Common, Tobe put himself to school. He sat on the primer bench with the little'uns and learned to read. Then he came up here and founded New Canaan."

"Good for him," the boy said. Freeman knew he was trying to put as much distance between himself and Running Tobe as possible. He was about to remind his grandson that Tobe was his direct blooded ancestor when the boy changed the subject. "You didn't say nothing about drawing down no dam this morning. You said we was going to dig up some dead people. I don't see no dead people."

Freeman suspected that the boy was trying to muster courage for what lay ahead. He said, "You'll do fine. You can help or watch or go fishing. This is mainly between me and them." "Them" was how Freeman referred to his people.

"I reckon I'll help. You'll be all in after five minutes, same as you are now. Say, can I keep a skull? To set up over the fireplace?"

Freeman smiled to himself. Keeping a skull to prove his courage by was just what Freeman would have wanted to do at his age. Freeman bent back over the pickpole and resumed circling the bull wheel like the mule in the song. The boy jumped from the railroad trestle onto the catwalk of the dam, something Freeman had repeatedly told him not to do. "Leave go of that pole before you bust a gut," he told his grandfather. He shouldered Freeman aside and took his place. A few months ago Freeman had quit wrestling with the boy. Over the past year he'd become too much for Freeman to handle and, Freeman suspected, was letting him win. The gate thunked into the top of its framework. It was as high as it went.

The 7:03 southbound came into sight on the spur track. As it approached the trestle it whistled twice to say good morning. Freeman and the boy waved. "One of these days I'm going to hop onto that train and never look back," the boy said.

"We can only hope so," Freeman said.

"Let's get a move on it," the boy said when the train had passed. Freeman knew he was still working on his courage.

"They ain't going anywhere," Freeman said. "Our people."

"Not ours. Yours."

Temporarily in ascendance, the boy was already standing in the skiff. Freeman handed down the pickax and two shovels and his grandfather's log-rolling peavey. "Get up in the bow," he told the boy. "I'll row."

"That's a very poor idea," the boy said. "Green around the gills as you are." Freeman was forever chiding his grandson that something he was fixing to do was a very poor idea. Green around the gills or not, Freeman enjoyed rowing a boat and intended to do so this morning, in the process regaining, however briefly, ascendancy over his grandson. Unlike raising a boy, rowing produced immediate and predictable results. Also rowing appealed to Freeman's temperament. You pulled the oars forward and the boat went backward.

They glided up the diminished impoundment past the stark white barkless trunks of drowned-out trees exposed by the receding water. The flooded-out shoreline forest stood silent—the bleached skeletons of some lost race of giants. As they entered the notch where the log drives had jammed, they could see the dark high-water marks on the cliffs overhead, from which Freeman had long ago been lowered in a basket. To the boy it appeared as though the cliffs were rising out of the water. Freeman thought of the Plimsoll lines on the grain freighters on which he'd traveled the world. Here in the notch there was a little current. Freeman feathered the oars to hold the skiff in place. "Look down," he said.

The boy peered over the side of the skiff. By degrees he made out, wavering in the green depths of the river, the fire-blackened shells of the stone houses and church of New Canaan. "My granddaddy was just a shaver when the Klan came riding," Freeman said. "Somehow he got away and hid out in the old logging camp upriver. The rest, nearly one hundred of them, were trapped inside the church."

For once the boy had nothing to say. "I've always suspicioned," Freeman told him, "that the true purpose of the dam was to put this out of sight and mind."

By then the boy had recovered himself. He spat onto the surface of the river and said, "He stopped too soon, I reckon. Running Tobe. He didn't run far enough."

"It's a shame you wasn't here to advise him," Freeman said.

"I'd have knowed better than to put down stakes in this hellhole," the boy said.

Freeman ran the bow of the skiff up onto a wet sandbar beside the narrowing river. A couple of dozen granite grave markers stood clustered nearby, Freeman and the boy got out of the skiff and walked through the stones. Aaron. Moses. Jincy. Orange. Tobias. Freeman said, "My granddaddy that escaped the fire told me his granddaddy, Running Tobe, said New Canaan wasn't home until they started burying their people here. All these graves date back before the fire. There wasn't enough left of the people inside the church to bury.

"These graves," Freeman continued, "are links between us and them. You may not think they're your people but they are. You wouldn't be here without them."

"Are we going to move them to dry ground or not?" the boy said.

"We are," Freeman said. But instead of going to the skiff for the shovels and pickax he sat down with his back against Tobe's marker.

"What is it?" the boy said.

"Listen to me" Freeman said. "I want you to—"

The boy never learned what his grandfather wanted him to do. The old man had sagged down against Tobe's stone. His chin rested on his chest. His eyes were still partly open and he was frowning as if in disapproval of some new similarity to himself that he'd just perceived in his grandson. At first the boy couldn't be sure. "You, sir," he said loudly near Freeman's ear.

The grandson half-expected a sour reply but for once the old man held his tongue.

"There," the boy said.

He went to the skiff and returned with the pickax and a long-handled shovel. Immediately he set to work. At first the soil was moist and sandy. Then hard bluish clay that required the pick. Once the boy glanced at his grandfather. The old man looked as though he was about to proclaim that all this was a very poor idea. Freeman was no midget but with the assistance of the peavey hook the boy rolled him over into the open grave. Filling it in was the work of half an hour.

The boy wrestled the skiff down over the sandbar to the river and got in and began to row, taking care to stay in mid-channel. Now the skeletal trees on the shorelines made him think of the remains of so many Negroes burned and hanged and whipped to death.

The boy scraped the skiff onto the exposed mud flats at the north end of the dam. He climbed up to the catwalk. There was the bull wheel with the pike impaled between its spokes. The gate creaked in its framework as the boy cranked it down. *The mule went around with its foot on the ground.* The day seemed to be moving backward.

Five miles away at the foot of the lake the evening north-bound whistled. The boy got his fishing knife out of his tackle box in case of tramps. He got the roll of bills out of the old man's McGinty jar. There was the paper they'd pinned to his shirt years ago. He left the paper in the jar.

The northbound was even shorter than usual. A snub-nosed diesel. Three empty pulp cars. Two boxcars. A caboose. It crept out onto the trestle. The door of one of the cars was partway open. The boy trotted alongside it but just before swinging aboard he changed his mind and a minute later the train was picking up speed as it headed north between the mountains and the lake.

At first light the next morning he nosed the launch up to the dock at the south end of the lake and cut the Johnson. The two sports, a well-preserved man who looked to be in his eighties and a somewhat younger man, perhaps his son, were waiting on the dock with their luggage and tackle. During the night the lake had turned itself over and the cold water had brought up the trout and salmon. The sports should have good fishing.

"Baker party?" the boy said.

"We thought Mr. Freeman would be here," the younger elderly man said in a friendly voice. "Is Mr. Freeman all right?"

"He's fine," the boy said. "Hand down your gear. We'll want to be fishing by sunup."

The younger elder helped the older one into the launch. They seemed like decent people and that was a relief. If you wound up with a couple of bellyachers it could be a long week.

The sports settled themselves in. Then the older man looked over his shoulder at the boy. "What should we call you?"

The boy restarted the Johnson. Then, swinging the launch into a tight semicircle and gunning it north up the lake: "Freeman. You can call me Freeman."

2

Where Is Don Quixote?

Elizabeth would have known what to do about the wind towers. Unfortunately, Kinneson's wife had passed a year ago. Passed where? Kinneson had no idea. From time to time he still heard her voice in his head, calm and practical, but thus far she had said nothing to him about the towers.

Elizabeth had been the one person whose opinion, other than Patchett's own, Patchett had the slightest regard for. On those occasions when Kinneson needed to get his hired man into gear, he'd say, "Liz told me we should cut the north hayfield today." Or, "Liz said this forenoon would be a good time to start tapping up back." Up back was the maple orchard on the ridge above the barn. As far as Kinneson knew, Patchett himself had never been married. Forty years ago he'd appeared at Kinneson's door out of a blizzard, sudden as a revenant, a young man with an old man's face. Elizabeth had fed him supper and he'd stayed on. In time he'd bought a thirdhand Airstream and set up housekeeping in it between the farmhouse and the hardtop road at the foot of the lane. A month after Patchett had quartered himself on them, Kinneson asked him a question. Was Patchett his first or last name? Patchett had given him a long slow wondering look and neither of them had broached the topic again.

Patchett might have known what to do about the wind towers himself. Now an old man with a young man's face, Patchett knew how to fix things. Given time enough, and someone to hand him tools and listen to him complain, Patchett could fix anything, from a broken flywheel on Kinneson's ancient Oliver tractor to the hard drive of the desktop computer Elizabeth kept the farm accounts on. Quite possibly Patchett could have fixed the wind towers. Fixed them, in some subtle and untraceable way, so that they'd never generate a single kilowatt of green power again. But a few weeks after Liz passed, Patchett had hooked his Airstream behind his pickup and lit out for Big Sky Country.

What had caused Patchett to jump ship, Montpelier'd made him take down his sign beside the hardtop road, claiming that it violated Vermont's anti-billboard legislation. Patchett had written to Montpelier, asking how a square of cardboard from a Mason shoe box with FISH WORMS FOR SALE and a hand-drawn arrow pointing up at his Airstream could qualify as a billboard. Montpelier did not reply so Patchett, seeing the handwriting on the wall, hit the high dusty, leaving the offending cardboard sign duct-taped to Kinneson's door with the message GONE FISHING printed just below the arrow. Patchett being Patchett he had not troubled himself to say where he had gone fishing. Ten days later Kinneson received a postcard from Gulch, Montana, depicting a range of snowcapped mountains that dwarfed Vermont's tallest peaks. It read: "I'm here. Patchett."

Kinneson had a grown son in Boston and a grown daughter
in New York. After Elizabeth passed and Patchett pulled up
stakes and went west, they urged him to unload the farm and
move closer to them. Kinneson abided his adult children, as
they did him, and enjoyed his grandkids, but if there was one
place he detested more than Boston, it was New York. The feel-
ing from Boston was mutual. His was the last working farm in
the township of Kingdom Common, and at eighty he couldn't
keep up with the twice-a-day regimen of milking one hundred
and fifty cows alone. Therefore, he hired two hardworking
Mexican brothers to help run his outfit. Mexicans were already
running most of the remaining farms in Kingdom County and,
as nearly as Kinneson could tell, running them more efficiently
than they had ever been run before. In Kinneson's estimation
the recent influx of Mexican workers was the best thing to happen to the Kingdom since his great-great-grandfather, James
Kinneson I, and a like-minded handful of James's neighbors,
had declared its independence from Vermont and the United
States and governed it as a freestanding republic for thirty years.

A few weeks after Kinneson hired on the Sanchez brothers,
the leach field below his farmhouse failed. Juan and Luis could
have put in a perfectly serviceable new one for the cost of several
truckloads of sand and gravel, a few hundred feet of PVC piping,
and the rental of a backhoe for half a day. Before they could get
started, someone—Kinneson suspected it was old man Potts
from over behind—reported the failure of his septic system
to the state authorities. In waltzed Montpelier again, this time
in the person of a spindling little know-it-all scarcely out of his
teens who called himself a sanitation hydrologist. Empowered
by an abrupt letter from some official or other, the hydrologist

made Kinneson install, to the tune of $18,500, a state-of-the-art septic system thirty feet long, twelve feet wide, and ten feet high, which in Kinneson's estimation could have accommodated half of the waste of the village of Kingdom Common. To pay for it he'd been constrained to cash in a whole life insurance policy whose proceeds, now that Elizabeth was gone, he'd intended to leave in trust with his son and daughter for his grandchildren.

Early one evening that summer Kinneson looked out his kitchen window over the top of the Indian burial mound, as he'd come to think of the new septic system, and saw four coyotes chasing a deer across the water meadow along the river. Before he could load his rifle they ran her down and tore her to pieces. The next morning a this-year's fawn still in its spots tottered into his barn-yard. Kinneson put the orphaned animal into an empty stall, where the coyotes couldn't get at it, and drove into the Common and bought a baby bottle. He coaxed the fawn into lapping a little warm milk off his fingers, then drinking from the bottle.

Against the advice of the Sanchez brothers, who had recently moved themselves and their families into two brand-new double-wides near the former site of Patchett's Airstream, Kinneson called the local game warden to report the killing of the doe and his discovery of the fawn. Over the phone line he heard a sound like a person sucking in air between his teeth. "I wish you hadn't told me that, Zeke," the warden said. The warden called his supervisor in St. Johnsbury, who called the head warden in Montpelier, who showed up at Kinneson's place the next morning with his two subordinates and ordered Kinneson to release the fawn back into the wild and let nature run its course. This Kinneson refused to do. The coyotes, who lived on the ridge up back, were nearly as large as the timber wolves their ancestors had interbred with, and fully as ferocious, and would snap up an unattended fawn within hours. The head warden shrugged and told his employees to get the deer out of the barn and let it go in the alders beside the river where, the following day, Kinneson came across its bloody hide and partially eaten hooves. Nature had run its course.

Above Kinneson's maple sugar orchard, along the ridgeline marking the west boundary of his property, a faint north-and-south-running trace cut through the woods, now mostly overgrown with hobblebush, gray birch, and striped maple. Nearby, at the top of the maple orchard, Kinneson and Elizabeth had placed a granite marker inscribed with their names and birth dates. Here their ashes would be buried in a single urn now containing Elizabeth's, which Kinneson kept in the pie safe in her former pantry. The trace, which was known as the Canada Post Road, and was owned by the township of Kingdom Common, had been built in 1812 by Kinneson's great-great-great-grandfather, Charles Kinneson I, whose aim it was to attack Canada and annex it to Kingdom County. In the event, Charles and his militia of would-be invaders were driven back across the border by a dozen angry *Quebecois habitants* armed with pitchforks and squirrel guns.

One afternoon Kinneson walked up through his maple trees to check on the grave marker. The stone stood where he'd left it, facing out over a prospect of most of the Kingdom. It was a beautiful place, but from just down the Post Road Kinneson heard voices. Through the underbrush he made out two men in white hard hats, coming his way with surveying instruments.

"Hello, old-timer," one of the surveyors called out. "What brings you up here?"

"My grandfather's great-grandfather built this road," Kinneson said. "What brings you up here?"

The surveyor handed Kinneson a business card with the words NORTHERN NEW ENGLAND GREEN POWER printed on it. He told Kinneson that his company planned to buy the Post Road from the township and erect twenty-one wind towers on it. There would be an information meeting at the town hall in Kingdom Common the following Thursday evening.

When Kinneson did not favor him with a reply, the surveyor said, "Well, no rest for the wicked," and made a dismissive gesture with the back of his hand, as if to shoo Kinneson off his own property. Kinneson's grandfather would have wrested the surveyor's transit out of his hands and given him a severe drubbing with it. His father, who made it a practice never to leave his house unarmed, would have run off the interlopers at gunpoint. This was a different era. As a rule Kinneson did not believe in taking the law into his own hands.

"Yes, sir, gentlemen," he said, and started back down the slope toward the farmhouse.

In general Ezekiel Kinneson regarded meetings, including Vermont's fabled grassroots town meetings, as a waste of time. In his view the sole purpose of meetings was to find reasons not to get things done. Patchett had disapproved of meetings, too. It was one of the few things they'd agreed on. Therefore, Kinneson's neighbors were surprised to see him at Thursday's information meeting. "When did you make bail, Z?" old man Potts brayed out at him as he entered the hall.

Green Power had hired a Burlington law firm specializing in litigating environmental issues. The firm's senior partner, a meticulous man in his sixties, offered the township of Kingdom Common $750,000 for a two-mile stretch of the Canada Post Road running along the ridge above Kinneson's farm. Kinneson paid little attention to the attorney as he nattered on and less attention yet to the speeches that followed, pro and con, from his fellow townspersons. When it was his turn to speak Kinneson rose and looked around the crowded hall and frowned. "See here," he said. "My name is Ezekiel Kinneson. I own the last working farm in this town. I milk one hundred and fifty cows, tap a thousand maple trees, fish the brooks that run off that ridge, and hunt along the Post Road. I am a seventh-generation Commoner who does not care to be told what to do or bribed into doing anything by anyone. For all these reasons I'm opposed to the towers."

Less than ten minutes later the town voted 245–181 in favor of selling the Post Road to the power company. Kinneson went home and wrote a two-page outraged letter relaying the news to Patchett. A week later he received a reply on one of Patchett's Big Sky postcards. The message read: "Blow them up come West."

Overnight word spread throughout the Kingdom, emanating from the post office like circles on a trout pond, that Kinneson had thrown in with a cadre of eco-terrorists. Report had it that he had driven to New Hampshire, where you could buy, with no questions asked, anything in the way of ordnance necessary to "live free or die," and purchased fifty-three cases of dynamite. Patchett himself was said to be posting east with a posse of mountain men to deal with the as-yet-nonexistent wind towers. The county prosecutor caught wind of the rumors and wangled an order from the district-court judge to send out the sheriff with Dr. Frannie Lafleur Kinneson, the local GP and three-afternoons-a-week consulting psychiatrist at the county hospital, to examine Kinneson and determine whether he had gone around the bend and become dangerous to himself or others.

Dr. Frannie, as she was universally referred to in the Kingdom, was Kinneson's great-niece by marriage. She had two grown sons herself but was still, in Kinneson's estimation, as cute as a button. She asked him the day of the week and his date of birth. Then she wanted to know the name of the president. Kinneson winked at her and said Abraham Lincoln. Dr. Frannie gave out a raucous belly laugh and snapped off her recording machine and said she only hoped that she'd be as sharp as Kinneson when she was eighty. The sheriff, John "Uncle Johnny" Kinneson, who detested the projected wind towers because they would destroy his secret deerstand on the Post Road, smiled and drove Dr. Frannie back to the village.

Several months passed. Everyone from Kinneson's grown children to the local postmistress who'd read Patchett's postcard and ignited the dynamite rumor had advised Ezekiel not to make any life-altering changes during his first year as a widower. Other than hiring on the Sanchez brothers, which Kinneson regarded as the smartest thing he'd done since marrying Elizabeth, he'd made no changes at all. Juan and Luis subscribed to several dairy-farming periodicals. They brought in agricultural consultants from the state university, and began looking into localvore projects such as beekeeping, cheese-making, and raising organically fed beef cattle. Their wives enrolled in community college courses, the children were well-mannered and studious. Kinneson enjoyed taking them fishing and playing catch with them. He liked thinking that they were the future face of the Kingdom and wished he could see the expression on old man Potts's face when they grew up to be selectpersons and road commissioners, school board members, deputy sheriffs, state legislators, members of Congress and, yes, presidents. One of the boys was a gifted ball-player. Kinneson envisioned him in pinstripes and a New York Yankees cap, pitching a no-hitter in Fenway Park.

In the late afternoons he sat out on the wraparound porch of the farmhouse where he'd sat evenings helping Elizabeth shell peas and cut up apples, and watched the towers rising ever higher on the ridge top.

"What do you look at, Grandfather?" the Sanchez children inquired.

"Those windmills up on the hill," Kinneson said.

"Why do you look at them?"

"Because they bear watching," Kinneson said. "Like you young scamps."

By August all twenty-one of the towers were in operation. They stood four hundred and sixty feet high. At night their red warning lights blinked on and off. More than half of the time their vast blades were motionless since the higher mountains immediately to the west blocked the prevailing wind. Nor, Kinneson had recently learned, could the antiquated electrical lines leading to and from the Kingdom accommodate more than half of what meager power they generated. Kinneson watched the wind blades not turning. He had never for one minute doubted what the scientists said about climate change, but the stationary blades would do little to combat it.

Throughout his life Kinneson had been an avid reader. After Liz passed he'd had trouble following anything longer than the court news or obituaries in the *Kingdom County Monitor*. He'd look out the window to check on the wind towers, then return to his book only to realize that he was rereading the page he'd just finished. One afternoon he found himself in the village library again. Ruth Kinneson, the librarian and Kinneson's second cousin by marriage, was boxing up some outdated westerns for an upcoming book sale.

"Welcome, stranger," Ruth said. "What do you hear from Mr. Patchett?"

For the briefest moment Kinneson wasn't sure who she meant. Ruth was the only person who ever referred to his former hired hand as Mr. Patchett.

"Not much," Kinneson said. "Since that penny postcard got all over town."

Ruth smiled. "Mr. Patchett is Mr. Patchett," she said. "I think he always felt the draw of the West."

She removed a book from the box: Zane Grey's *Riders of the Purple Sage*. There was Patchett's name on the check-out card, printed neatly a dozen or so times.

"Mr. Patchett read and reread every one of these books," Ruth said. "I'm sure you knew that."

Kinneson had known no such thing. He wondered what else there might be about Patchett that he didn't know. After that day many years ago when he had inquired about Patchett's name, he had never asked him a personal question. Now, looking at Patchett's block printing on the library card, he realized that his friend had not been fleeing anything, including Montpelier and its thousand and one regulations, when he'd struck out for Montana. Rather, Patchett had been realizing a lifelong dream. At that moment, Kinneson knew exactly what he must do.

That evening he summoned the Sanchez brothers to the farmhouse kitchen. Without preamble he said that he was prepared to sell them his seven hundred and sixty acres, the barn and livestock, and the machinery, at assessed or book value. He would hold the mortgage himself, zero percent interest and no down payment. After his death, the monthly payments would go to his son and daughter. He would retain the farmhouse and two acres for his children and grandchildren to use as a getaway. Juan and Luis thanked him and said they would keep up the place, of which Kinneson had no doubt. He enjoyed thinking of old man Potts's consternation when he learned that the last working farm in the township was now owned by Mexicans.

The brothers returned to their trailers to share the news with their wives. Immediately Kinneson began packing. He wouldn't need much. His fly rod, deer rifle, winter clothing, and boots. He could bunk in with Patchett, he figured, until he found a place of his own. Late that afternoon he'd brought the grave marker from the maple orchard down off the ridge on a stoneboat behind his Oliver and gee-hawed it up into the bed of his pickup. He didn't sleep much that night. Except for a year in Korea when he was in the service, he'd spent only a few nights away from his own bed. Now he was leaving the Kingdom forever. He imagined that he could hear the low throbbing hum of the windmills. Once he heard Elizabeth say, very distinctly,

"A red-and-yellow grasshopper fly, fished wet, is a good bet out there this time of year."

He was up at first light. He limited himself to one cup of coffee so he wouldn't have to stop five times before he was out of Vermont. He removed the urn containing Liz's ashes from the pie safe and wrapped it in his hunting jacket and stashed it in the bottom of the toolbox behind the pickup cab. The rig coughed, ground out, coughed again, and started. He'd have Patchett throw in a rebuilt starter when he arrived.

The river was invisible in the September mist. Higher on the ridge the clouds had dispersed. In the rising sun the twenty-one wind towers lit up as red as Armageddon and the fiery blades began to turn like the big and little wheels of Ezekiel's biblical namesake. Well before he reached the hardtop road where Patchett had started all this with his fish worms sign, Kinneson knew that, for him, Big Sky Country was no solution.

"How was Montana?" Juan called to him a minute later as he pulled back into his dooryard.

"Montana's all right if you like it," Kinneson said. "It isn't the Kingdom."

Still, Kinneson realized, as he returned Elizabeth's ashes to the pantry, that it was not his beloved green fields or hundred-year-old sugar bush or six generations of forebears that had changed his mind about leaving the Kingdom. What brought him back was the wind towers. Looking up at their blades, looming high above the county in the mild fall sunlight like so many winged alabaster idols, Kinneson pursed his lips. As he'd told the Sanchez children, the towers bore watching. It had fallen to him to watch them. That might not be much but it was the one thing left in his world that he was certain of.

3

Good Sam Merryton

Two dilapidated churches sat across the street from the south end of the village green. Between them was a vacant lot. The churches had once been the heart and soul of the village. They were crowded to capacity, not just on Christmas Eve and Easter but each Sunday morning. Infants were christened at their marble baptismal fonts, couples married at their altars. Funeral sermons were preached over the beloved, and not so beloved, departed.

For as long as the townspeople could remember, rivalry between the two congregations had been the order of the day. They vied for the largest Sunday school and choir, the most scholarly minister, the best-appointed parsonage. Each congregation fielded its own baseball team. The winner of the annual Old Home Day game between the Congregationalists and the Presbyterians posted the score on the bulletin board in front of their church and left it up all year.

Each congregation owned a much cherished possession.

In a floor safe in the minister's study of the Congregational church was a communal service from the Revere Silver Works, said to have been cast by Paul Revere himself. An antiques dealer from Boston had offered the Congo elders eighteen thousand dollars for the silver service, but selling it was out of the question. The same dealer had hinted that he might go as high as fifty thousand for the two-hundred-year-old copper weathervane in the shape of a native brook trout atop the steeple of the Presbyterian church. The Presby elders were outraged by the very idea that they would ever consider parting with Sir Izaak Walton, as the copper trout had long ago been named. Not only was the fish an emblem of their faith, it was well known, at least to many of the older Commoners, that Sir Izaak knew in advance when a front was approaching Kingdom County. Often he would begin to swing around in that direction a day before the weather arrived. Sell Izaak Walton? The Presbyterians would as soon sell their souls.

Over the years, as the family farms of the county began to go under and the young people left for college or jobs on the other side of the hills and returned only for short visits, both congregations dwindled. By degrees the churches fell into disrepair. There was little money to replace leaky roofs, flaking paint, and frayed electrical wiring. Chimney swifts nested in the belfreys. There was a time where the empty lot between the two houses of worship had been kept mowed as close as the ball diamond on the village green. Recently the lot had grown up to burdocks and Canadian bull thistles, blackberry brambles, and thorn apples. It had become a haven for rats, blue-and-yellow-striped garter snakes, and feral cats.

MINISTER NEEDED read the white letters on the bulletin

board of first one church, then the other. For a time they limped along with interns still in seminary and fill-in ministers hailed out of retirement. One venerable supply pastor renowned for his waggish sense of humor looked out over the dozen stalwart worshipers scattered through the pews of the Congregational church one wintry Sunday morning and said, "Well, folks, I guess what they say about Protestants is true. You can get them to do anything but go to church."

While the congregations continued to diminish, the rivalry between the churches did not. From time to time a few "mixed marriages" took place. In those cases the dauntless couples usually exchanged vows and attended services in the bride's church. Also, the Congos and Presbys shared a cemetery on the east edge of the village. If asked, most members of the two congregations would probably concede that they would dwell in the same hereafter. No doubt they would attend different churches there, as well.

Ministers who tried to heal the rift between the feuding congregations met with little success, and soon moved on. Kingdom Common was notoriously hard on clergymen in general. Someone was always looking over their shoulder, or worse yet, their wife's. One young Congo pastor told Editor Jim Kinneson that, in the eyes of his congregation, he had not done one thing right since coming to the Common. His wife had threatened to go home to her mother if he did not resign by the end of the year.

One evening not many years ago, in lilac time in the Kingdom, Editor Jim Kinneson and his brother and fishing partner, Judge Charlie Kinneson, were fly-fishing the long pool in the Lower Kingdom River behind the vacant lot between the churches known in the Common as the "church hole" or, simply, as "church." They were standing about sixty feet apart, casting number-eighteen Adams dry flies and hoping to lure out the trophy brown trout that had claimed the church hole for itself three years ago, devouring or driving away every other fish in the pool.

"Not tonight, brother," Charlie finally said.

Jim nodded. He reeled in, hooked his Adams in the cork handle of his Orvis Battenkill, and turned to head up the low bank. That's when he noticed the strangers. They were standing in the vacant lot between the churches, a man and a woman. Parked on the street nearby was a battered van hitched to a canvas-covered trailer. The man wore a rusty black suit and scuffed dress shoes. He was middle-aged, middle-sized, dark-complected, with tired eyes. Around his neck he wore a preacher's collar, threadbare and yellowing, and he was holding an old-fashioned carpetbag with smooth wooden handles. There he stood, enveloped in his own silence, looking a little shopworn, frowning down at the brothers as if he'd just come across their names in the court news of the *Kingdom County Monitor*.

The woman beside him was tall and slender with elongated, delighted green eyes and long hair the shade of light maple sugar. She wore a close-fitting yellow sundress and matching heels, and looked a good twenty years younger than her companion. There was just enough light left in the sky for Jim to read, stenciled in red letters on the side of the van, the following words:

The Right Rev. Dr. Samuel Merryton
Church of the Holy Trinity
Revivals $50

Revelations $75

Resurrections $100 and Up

"Evening," Jim called out to the strangers.

The story—it was all over town by nine o'clock the next morning—was that the frowning newcomer in the clerical collar said, "Cast in your line again, oh ye of little faith." This Jim refuted half a dozen times until he could see that no one was going to believe him. What the man had actually said was: "Try it again, bub. Throw in over across where the current sets in close to the far bank."

Jim grinned. So did his brother. "You heard the man, bub," Charlie said. "Do what he told you."

Jim shrugged. "Well, it's a good evening to fish a little longer. Whether they're biting or not."

"Any evening's a good evening to fish," the stranger said. "You'll see. You hook him, I'll land him for you."

Jim waded back into the river, uncorked his fly, and flicked it upstream and across the current, keeping his rod tip high so the slack in his line wouldn't drag the fly under. It was almost too dark to make out the tiny Adams floating down the choppy surface of the water. The fish struck with a hard *pop* and Jim set the hook.

For the next twenty minutes the editor played the big trout up and down the church pool. Once he looked back over his shoulder. The strangers had made their way across the lot to stand beside Charlie and watch the battle from the top of the bank. Jim noticed that the pretty young woman had removed her heels and was standing in the field in her stocking feet. "Careful, miss," he said. "Watch out for broken glass." She smiled and waved in acknowledgment. When she bent forward to slip on her heels and her blond hair fell alongside her face, she looked scarcely out of her teens.

Meanwhile, the trout was beginning to tire. Soon it was spent. Its head was partway out of the water as Jim, the Orvis bent nearly double, skidded it toward the gravel bar he was standing on.

"Hold up," the preacher said. "I'll he'p you land that big boy."

He came down the bank and grabbed Jim's leader three or four feet above the fly embedded in the corner of the trout's mouth and horsed the hooked fish toward the bar. The trout's bright yellow belly and the dime-sized red spots on its sides glowed in the last light of the evening. It was larger than Jim had thought, six or perhaps even seven pounds. In a final desperate flurry it flopped out of the water and fell twisting back with its full weight on the leader, which snapped in two just above the fly like pack thread. The fish shot off with its dark back out of the shallow water. A moment later it vanished into the depths of the pool.

"Gone," the stranger said in a grim voice. "Gone with the wind."

Charlie laughed but the stranger shook his head. "Ain't that just the way of the world?" he said. "Howsoever it may be in other worlds, ain't that just the way of this one?" He turned to the young woman beside him. "Isn't that so, sis?"

"Oh, yes, Brother Samuel," she said in a lilting voice.

"Yes, sir," the preacher said. Then, "I'm not telling you what to do, friend, but you need a stronger line. Yours is as frail as mortal man when tempted by our one great enemy. Is it true?"

"Is what true?" Jim said.

"What that sign says out front of the church. 'Minister Needed.'"

"Actually we need two ministers," Charlie said. "Trouble is, we can't afford them."

"Well, now," said the wayfarer. "It just so happens I does me a little preaching now and again. Look here."

From his satchel he produced a hard-used Bible, which he handed to Jim. "You hold the Book on me," he said. "Open her up to any text whatsoever, prefer the New to the Old but either will answer. Prompt me chapter and verse. I'll recite."

Jim opened the Bible. In the twilight he could just make out, stamped on the inside of the front cover, the words "Property of the Salvation Army, Macon, Georgia. Do not remove from these premises."

Jim riffled through the pages. "Ecclesiastes 12:12," he said.

" 'Of making many books there is no end,'" the preacher said. " 'Nother way of saying all is vanity. Specially book writing."

Charlie pointed at Jim. "He's a book writer."

"There you have it," the stranger said.

Jim handed back the Bible. He was still nettled with the preacher for breaking off his fish. He suspected that the man might have done it on purpose to demonstrate the way of the world and the frailty of mankind.

"Which congregation do you plan on approaching?" Jim said. "Congregationalists or Presbyterians?"

"Both," the stranger said, extending his hand. "The Right Reverend Dr. Samuel T. Merryton, aka Good Sam Merryton. This here's my kid sister, Sister Gloryanne Merryton. Sister

Gloryanne is a youth pastor on temporary leave from her mission in Africa. Today is your lucky day, gentlemen. You have lost a fish and found a fisher of men. Your pastoral search is over."

"How's it hurt any other body for Sam to put up a tent on a empty lot and preach an old-fashioned Bible sermon?" Sam said the next morning in his rather high-pitched, querulous voice. He was tipped back in a chair with his shoes on the conference table in the Harmony Room of the Presbyterian Church, holding court to several elders from each congregation. Editor Jim Kinneson, sitting beside his brother Charlie across the table from Sam, noticed a hole the size of a fifty-cent piece in the sole of his right shoe. He was tapping his toe to the strains of Scott Joplin's "The Entertainer," as rendered in a spirited fashion by his sister Gloryanne on the piano in the adjacent Sunday school primer room.

Elder George Quinn Jr. said, "Well, Reverend Merryton, that lot between the churches is private property. We Presbyterians own half of it, the Congos own the other half. You didn't ask either church for permission."

"I would've," Sam said. "Only I was a-scart you'd say no."

Even George laughed at such an innocuous reply. But Sam reared back in his chair and said, "Seem to me like that lot *God*'s property. I asked God for permission. God say, 'Fine, Sam. Long as you going about my bidness, you go right on ahead and set up shop wherever you want to."

Sam swung his feet down off the table and stood up. "I tell you what," he said. "I'll step out of the room, give you boys some privacy to decide. One little revival meeting tonight can't hurt. Your two churches can split the offering, you need it worse than Sam."

Sam winked at Jim and Charlie and went into the primer room, leaving the door open a crack.

"I don't know about this fella," Elder George Quinn Jr. said. "He certainly isn't from around here."

"Neither are four and a half billion other people," Judge Charlie Kinneson said.

"He doesn't even speak like a white man," Tanager Davis, a Congo deacon, said.

"I does when the occasion calls for it," Sam said. "When the occasion calls for it, I can sling and fling the King's English with they best of them." He seemed to have manifested himself back at the conference table again, much the way he and Gloryanne had appeared on the riverbank the evening before. "Moreover, you'll not find me deficient in my familiarity with sacred chapter and verse. A brief demonstration."

He reached into his carpetbag and pulled out the swiped Bible, which he handed across the table to Jim. "If you please, editor," he said.

Jim opened the Bible. "Luke 5:6," he said.

" 'And when they had let down their nets, they enclosed a great multitude of fishes; and their net brake,' " Sam said. "Same as I show these two old boys last night on the river. Sam catch any kind of fish you name outen a cracked teacup. Fisher of fish, fisher of men. Now I gone show you how to build a new church. No charge."

"Sounds good to me," Judge Charlie said. "I move we let Sam do his show."

"Discussion?" George Quinn Jr. said.

"We won't tolerate any kind of rumpus," Perley Benson said. "That would have to be understood from the outset."

"No shouting, no thumping, no talking in tongues," Sam agreed. "Does I look like the kind of fella gone dandle poisonous vipers and yell out jabberwocky?"

Jim cut his eyes at his brother. The Right Reverend Dr. Samuel Merryton looked exactly like the kind of preacher who spoke in tongues and waved rattlesnakes in the air.

"What's that 'Resurrection' business painted on the doors of your van all about?" George said. "You don't really claim to bring back dead folks?"

"I just slapped that on to rouse curiosity," Sam said. "Oncet I gave mouth-to-mouth to a billy goat got himself zapped by a Weed Chopper 'lectric fence."

The elders and deacons shook their heads. But they seemed to have made up their minds that Sam Merryton was harmless. In the end they gave him permission to do three shows, one a week for each of the next three weeks starting that evening. In an access of goodwill the Presbyterian elders offered to let him and Gloryanne stay in their empty parsonage across from the north end of the green.

"Best decision you ever made, gentlemen," Sam said. "I sees y'all tonight at the revival. Seven sharp."

For his revival Sam optimistically borrowed one hundred folding metal chairs from the town hall. He hired several junior-high boys playing ball on the common to lug them over to his open-sided pavilion on the lot between the churches. The boys raced through the rows of chairs, ungovernable as young orang-

utans. "WWE chair fight!" they shouted, and began to men-
ace at one another with steel chairs.

"Future face of America," Sam said to Jim.

From the trailer behind his van Sam fetched a faded hand-
lettered sign. In tall red letters it said: OLD-FASHIONED REVIVAL
MEETING TONIGHT 7 P.M.

Sam returned to the trailer and brought forth a can of paint
and a brush. Below the time on the sign he painted, in the same
fire-engine-red letters, BENEFIT OF THE FIRST UNITED CHURCH
OF KINGDOM COUNTY.

"Good evening, brothers and sisters," Sam said. "My name is
the Right Reverend Dr. Samuel Merryton, a-k-a Good Sam
Merryton."

To Editor Jim Kinneson, the itinerant evangelist looked seed-
ier than ever. About fifty curiosity-seekers sat scattered inside
the pavilion. From the trailer Sam had produced two banks of
floodlights, which he'd hung from poles at the front of the open
tent. A jumper cable stretched from the battery of the running
van to the floodlights. Sam stood on an orange crate flanked
by the glaring lights. At his feet was his old-fashioned carpetbag. On a crate beside Sam stood Gloryanne, tall in her high
heels, wearing a short red dress, her hair glowing in the floodlights. From a strap around her neck hung a beat-up accordion.
The air inside the pavilion smelled like mildewed canvas, tram-
pled grass, hot lights, stale sweat, and fresh running water from
the nearby river.

Sam nodded at Gloryanne, who played a bar of "Onward
Christian Soldiers" on the accordion. "Good Christian soldiers,"

Sam said, reaching into his carpetbag and withdrawing the Salvation Army Bible. He handed the Bible to Sister Gloryanne and said, "Sis, take and open this holy book and let God guide you to a text for this evening's sermon."

The beautiful youth missionary smiled angelically, though Editor Jim Kinneson thought he detected that same hint of delighted laughter in her eyes that he'd noticed on the evening he and Charlie first encountered her and Sam on the riverbank. "Our scripture reading for tonight comes from the Book of Mark, chapter 3, verse 25."

" 'And if a house be divided against itself, that house cannot stand,' " Sam said. "Hear, now, o Israel, the Parable of the House Divided. Two Kingdom County families lived on neighboring farms and despised one another. No one knew why. Always been that way. But the black-eyed, long-legged gal from one family fell in love with the young man next door. Hand in hand, up they go to the old folks and ask permission to join in holy matrimony. Whoa, Nellie! Old folks horrified. Not over they dead body. Fine. Young couple elope, run off to Malibu, multiply and increase and flourish. Back home in the hills, no young folks left to milk the moo cows, feed the red chickens. Good people, those two side-by-side farms began to run downhill fast. The more the old folks fuss and feud and blame each other, the closer the wolf get to the door. Then one day the young folks and gran'chirren appear out of the blue. Dear Lord and Master, the elders hugged they neck and wept for joy. The two farms joined together and prospered again. United they thrive, divided they fall into receivership.

"Now, then," Sam continued. "Those two farms, they be the two churches of your village. The old generation, they

the church elders. That black-eyed gal and her handsome
swain the young folks this town. United they stand. Your two
churches got to combine into one. Here endeth the Parable
of the House Divided. Loosen up your purse strings, best
beloved. We about to take up a collection to build that one
church."

Sam stepped off the orange crate and picked up his carpetbag. Holding it open by its handles, he made his way slowly up
and down the aisles through the sparse audience as Gloryanne
sang, in her lilting soprano voice, accompanied by the wheez-
ing accordion, the old offertory thanksgiving: "Praise God from
whom all blessings flow . . ."

When she finished, Sam began to chant out in a singsong
manner, like a carnival barker, "Round and round the satchel
go, where she stop, nobody know. Pony up, folks. We got us a
shining tabernacle to build."

Jim dropped a five-dollar bill into the satchel. Charlie added
a ten-spot. Most people contributed a few coins or a crumpled
dollar bill or two.

When he finished taking up the offering Sam returned to
his station between the floodlamps and stepped back up on the
orange crate. He peered into the satchel and shook his head.
"For shame," he said. "You the ones reap the blessing of the
new church. Let's try this again, folks. Practice makes perfect."

Once again Sam made his progress through the chairs.
"Sorry," Charlie said. "I gave at the office."

Again Sam gave the contents of the satchel a doleful look.
He sifted the bag from side to side like a man panning for gold.
The handful of change inside jingled faintly. Sam frowned and
shook his head. Then abruptly he lifted the carpetbag over his

head and turned it upside down. Out poured a ringing cascade of newly minted quarters, fifty-cent pieces, and silver dollars. Crisp, new five-, ten-, and twenty-dollar bills fluttered down in the wake of the shining coins. "Multiplied," Sam said in a matter-of-fact tone of voice. "Signifying the revival of hope for a united tabernacle.

"I hope to see this congregation multiplied likewise," Sam continued. "I hope to see it multiplied many times over a week from tonight at the 'Revelation' meeting. Come one, come all, Sam gone reveal to you how we make one church from two. May the Lord bless you and keep you and make his heavenly light to shine down upon you, folks, and I sees you in a week. Bring your pocketbooks. New churches don't come free."

The next morning at 9:00 sharp Sam, carpetbag in hand, was the first customer through the door of the Bank of Kingdom Common, where he opened an account for the United Church building fund in his name, George Quinn's, and Tanager Davis's. On an eight-foot-long plank donated by Benson's hardware Sam painted a facsimile of an outdoor thermometer, which he likewise labeled UNITED CHURCH BUILDING FUND. Beside the top of a short red arrow he inscribed the amount of his first bank deposit: $384.18, most of which was his own seed money. He propped up the plank against his van in the lot between the churches.

From the elders and deacons Sam wangled lists of the current members of the two faltering congregations. He talked the church fathers into checking off the names of comfortably situated parishioners, and spent the next several days soliciting contributions for the building fund.

It turned out that the evangelist was handy with tools. He could silence a banging screen door, do a little plumbing, bring back to life an old car that hadn't run in years. "Jesus was a carpenter," he liked to tell the widows and elderly maiden ladies he assisted. He had a knack for drawing stories out of them about the olden days, and encouraged the widows to make hefty donations to the fund in the names of their deceased husbands or sons who'd gone off to war and fallen in battle. In the long summer evenings after supper he swatted flies and grounders to kids on the common and regaled them with stories about his glory days pitching for a barnstorming Christian baseball team. He claimed to have struck out both Joe DiMaggio and Ted Williams in exhibition games.

One day Jim and Charlie took Sam brook-trout fishing on Pond Number Three in the wilderness just south of the Canadian border. Using an old cane pole he'd discovered in a closet at the parsonage, and garden worms for bait, Sam caught two trout for every one landed by the fly-fishing brothers.

Meanwhile word had traveled through the village like sap rising up maple trees in the spring that Sister Gloryanne Merryton was in the early stages of pregnancy. It was whispered that the father of the baby was a fourteen-year-old boy she'd seduced during her youth ministry on the Upper Limpopo River. Jim's wife, Dr. Frannie Lafleur Kinneson, whom Sister Gloryanne had consulted earlier in the week, told Jim that this rumor was as preposterous as it was vicious.

"Well, just how did she manage to get pregnant then?" Jim said.

Frannie winked at her former high school sweetheart, now her longtime husband. "Come upstairs with me, James. I'll show you exactly how."

"Now, people," Sam told the overflowing crowd at the second tent meeting, after the preliminary hymns and prayers. "Tonight I gone show you a genuine revelation. All this past week people stop old Sam on the street, buttonhole him on the village green and say, 'Sam you got a fund-raiser going, all well and fine. But how does you propose to build a new church for five, six thousand dollars? Or say you renovate one church, bring it up to code? Which church you renovate, which you raze to the ground? That a recipe for outright war. Hatfields and McCoys ain't nothing to it. So what we gone do? Once again, let us turn to God's Book."

From the magic satchel, Sam removed his Bible, which he seemingly opened at random. "Mark again," he said in a surprised voice. "Mark 2:21. 'No man seweth a piece of new cloth on an old garment.' That what Scripture say, all right. But what God trying to reveal to us here?"

Sam paused and the people leaned forward to hear God's revelation to them. Gloryanne played an anticipatory riff on her accordion.

"We know what Scripture saying here," Sam repeated. "But sometimes we got to look at what Scripture don't say. And what old Mark don't say, Mark nor God neither, is that two old garments cannot be sewed together to make one piece of strong cloth. Don't we have two old tabernacles? We do. Where does Scripture say we can't use the sturdy beams and rafters and granite foundation blocks, yes, even the furnishings from two old churches to build one new church?"

A murmur of interest rippled through the crowd. Sam gave his patented Sullivan nod to all quarters of the audience. "People always asking me," he said, " 'Dr. Merryton, what you did before you was a preacher?' And I say, 'I grew up a carpenter and the son of a carpenter.' Therefore, I will show you how to dismantle your two churches and join them together into one great tabernacle. Let no man put asunder what we have joined together. And yea, Izaak Walton, the copper trout, will stand vigil over the one church, which will celebrate communion in the Revere silver service. And now let us pass the satchel for the offering because there will still be new paint to purchase, and wiring, plumbing and insulation and a good furnace, also they new minister's salary, that's me."

When the satchel at last came back to Sam, standing in the hissing lights at the front of the pavilion, he peered inside and nodded. "Amazing," he said.

Sam paused. "Nothing short of amazing," he said again. He turned to Gloryanne and raised his arms like a symphony conductor. Accompanied by the ailing accordion, she and Sam sang " 'Amazing Grace, how sweet thou art, to save a wretch like me.' "

"That's right," Sam continued, "a wretch like me. Next week, at 'Resurrection,' I will tell you how Sam, the biggest, backslidingest wretch of all, committed all seven deadly sins and some new ones besides, until he saw the light and was reborn, yes, resurrected, just as we will resurrect Sunday worship in this village. 'Til then, may the Lord bless and keep you and let His light to shine upon you."

• • •

"That's the last we'll see of that old boy and his moll," Judge Charlie said to Jim on their way out of the pavilion that evening. But so far from absconding with the building fund and the hefty offering from the second tent meeting, Sam entrusted the contents of the carpetbag to George Quinn Jr. to deposit at the bank the next morning.

One evening that week Sister Gloryanne gave a slideshow presentation at the Presbyterian church on her work in Africa. One slide depicted the beautiful young missionary surrounded by a multitude of small black children in brightly colored choir robes. In the background across a two-lane asphalt highway was a billboard that read BUTCH'S TRANSMISSION REPAIR, BIRMINGHAM AL. Once a month the congregation took up a collection for its foreign missions. This month it would go to Sister Gloryanne's Church of the Upper Limpopo. When the Congos learned of their rivals' largesse, they doubled their donation.

In the meantime Sam continued his lucrative home visits. The red arrow of the building-fund thermometer crept up to three, then four, then five thousand dollars. Miss Elizabeth Anderson, the ninety-year-old heiress of the American Heritage Furniture fortune, wrote the United Church Fund a check for ten thousand dollars. It was decided to donate the entire proceeds of the annual Old Home Day on the village common to the fund. Somehow, the two churches scraped together enough players to field teams for the final interdenominational baseball game, which Sam umpired. With the score tied 7–7 at the end of nine innings, and two hours of good daylight left, Sam called the game. What a howl went up. Partisans from each side began to mill around on the infield. Shoving matches broke out. "Clear the field," Sam shouted. "You're tossed out of here, all of you, kit and caboodle." He shot his right arm over his head, index finger extended. Jim got a photograph for that week's *Monitor* of Sam throwing both congregations off the ball diamond. He captioned the melee DIVIDED WE FALL. Below the photograph was a closeup shot of the fund-raiser thermometer at $15,000: UNITED WE STAND.

Meanwhile it was reported that late at night rock and roll music and loud laughter had been heard coming from the parsonage. Queried about the goings-on, Sam said that he and Gloryanne were holding Bible study meetings. Glory cooked a chicken-and-biscuit dinner for the seniors of the village and charged the fixings to the Presbyterian church. The elders called Sam onto the carpet and scolded him for turning the parsonage into a soup kitchen.

"Good Sam's just preparing a place at the table for the least of these," the evangelist said.

"Well, the trouble is, Sam, it's our table and your sister bought the food on our dime," George Quinn said.

"No, sir, begging your pardon," Sam said. "It God's table and God's food and God's dime. Come one, come all to the tent meeting tonight. Called 'Resurrection.' Resurrect you sorry selves for telling Sam and the nice young blond-headed missionary lady not to feed they codgers. Case closed, world without end amen."

That evening the entire vacant lot between the two churches was packed with people. Sam mounted his orange crate and said, "Listen here, fellow mourners. I gone tell you what a abandoned wretch Sam was. Oh, yeah. He the worst wretch in all Waycross County. Give in to ardent drink. Cast eyes on the neighbor's wife and comely nineteen-year-old daughter. Roll dice, gamble at cards. Take the name of the Lord thy God in vain, steal from the poor box, lose he own good wife and babies."

Sam nodded at Sister Gloryanne, who sang out in her sweet clarion voice, "He once was lost," accompanied by a bar on the accordion.

"I once was lost," Sam trolled out. "I was a lost lamb. Then one night on the road to the Red Lantern Inn in Damascus— that's Damascus, Georgia—ripping along down the trace comes a big blue ball of 'lectricity. That fiery ball roll up the Red Lantern, drunkards and all. Then it make straight for Sam. Sam, he turn tail and run but the ball overtake him and rolls him up inside and plunks him out at the churchhouse door. Sam's hair stood on end and his eyes bug out. Not out of the woods yet, though. Got blue sparks jumping off all ten of his fingers, blue sparks spewing out of his mouth. 'Mr. God,' says Sam, 'I hearby swears that from this moment on, I, Samuel Merryton, will dedicate my life to going about your bidness. Just tell me what it is you want me to do.'

"And lo! a booming voice rent the sky. It say, 'Sam, go north. Go north to Kingdom Common, up Canady way. Go north, my son, up they boondocks.'

"So I say, 'Lord, Lord, whyever you want me to venture to Canady? Can't grow a red tomato or a nice ripe ear of corn up there to save your blessed soul.'

"And God spake out the fireball, 'That where my bidness is, Sam. Got two squabbling churches up there need to be

united. Tear down the two buildings and raise up one tabernacle.'

"Our text for this evening is Ecclesiastes 3:1," Sam continued. " 'To everything there is a season.' This the season to tear
down the old and build up the new. Why wait? This afternoon
I see Izaak Walton up top the church steeple start to shift into
the west. Old Mr. Izaak, he knows which way the wind blow,
knows a storm coming. We got one more day of good weather,
then Katie bar the door! Sunup tomorrow, good people. Down
come the old, up go the new. Resurrection Day arrive in Kingdom Common. Sis?"

" 'Turn, turn, turn,' " Gloryanne sang, her voice soaring
into its uppermost register.

" 'Turn, turn,' " chimed in the congregation as the magic
carpetbag started its rounds. " 'A time to laugh, a time to
weep.' "

Jim glanced at his brother. Charlie gave him a somber look.
Then he winked.

Swept along by the evangelist's enthusiasm, the church fathers
agreed to dismantle the two houses of worship on the following
day, before the storm arrived. Two local building contractors,
one from each congregation, would supervise the work.
Sam served as overall clerk of the works. To lift the steeples
from their moorings, he had rented a ninety-foot-tall crane
from Memphremagog. Men with roaring chain saws severed
the two-by-six hemlock collars spiking the belfreys to the wall
plates. The crane plucked off the steeples intact, setting them
side by side on the riverbank like the severed turrets of two

haunted castles. Their gray-and-maroon slate shingles could be reused to roof the new steeple. Out came the old wood-burning stoves. They would be replaced by a baseboard electrical heating system. Up with the tough elm floorboards, the square-headed old nails screeching like owls. Izaak Walton was locked with the silver Revere communal service in the safe from the former Congregationalist church.

Sam was here, there, everywhere, chivvying both work forces to compete with each other like two rail-laying teams racing toward a common destination. Beams, rafters, and joists, some with the overlapping adze marks visible where they'd been hewed to size, were stacked in the vacant lot. The maple pews from the Presbyterian church were piled up with the white-ash pews seven generations of Congos had polished with the sanctified seats of their Sunday raiment. Gingerly, the leaded stained-glass windows from the Congo church and the plain windows from the Presbyterian church were carried over to the basement of the town hall for temporary storage. Through his bullhorn Sam shouted, "From two old tabernacles cometh one new cathedral, folks. The cedars of Lebanon wasn't nothing to these hallowed old planks."

"This heap of junk look like Solomon's temple to you, bud?" Charlie said to Jim. They'd been crowbarring yellow-birch wainscoting off the inside walls of the Presbyterian church, trying not to splinter the thin paneling.

"Where do you think all this is heading?" Jim asked his brother.

"The same place you think it's headed," Charlie said. "Into one of your stories."

Two dump trucks on loan from the township of Kingdom

Common went back and forth between the demolition site and the county landfill, loaded with plaster and lath, cardboard boxes full of Sunday school tracts, church programs decades old, tattered disused hymnals, cracked flower vases, even a bundle of unsigned handwritten sermons from nobody knew how long ago. Editor Kinneson saved out, to present to the local historical society, a tall black ledger listing the names of chronic Presbyterian backsliders who'd been "churched" for various offenses. He showed Charlie two entries in which, as a young man, their great-great-grandfather, Charles Kinneson II, had been churched for racing his team of driving Morgans to and from Sunday services.

At noon Sister Gloryanne Merryton served a bean-hole bean dinner at the town hall for all comers. Sam and Glory sat on the stage at the head table with the elders and their wives. Sam stood to ask the blessing. He lifted his right hand heavenward and said, "Hearken, o Israel, to the Parable of Good Sam Merryton. Off in the forests of Canady was a end-of-the-line burg in the middle of nowhere. Once this village had a thriving furniture factory and a bustling railroad. It was surrounded by prosperous farms. Had it two active churches and two winning ball teams. Nice Grange hall. Famous Academy. No more. Factory close, railroad shut down, can't keep the churches open and desperate for a minister. Up comes a rich old retired preacher to scope out the job. Takes one look at the rundown churches, drives right on round the village green and out of town without even stopping. Next a young minister fresh out of seminary comes to town. Whoa, Nellie! Ain't got no Starbucks, ain't got no Gold's Gym, ain't got no cineplex or five-star restaurant. Back he goes faster than he drive up. But who this old boy poking up the road? I do believe it none other than the Right Reverend Dr. Samuel Merryton. Old slow-walking, slow-talking Sam. He don't see two rundown churches. He sees one new flourishing church. Where we building the new United Church? Right plumb beside the river is where."

Sam turned to Gloryanne. "Sis, take us on home with 'Come Let's Gather by the River.' Then we'll eat."

The afternoon sped by. About three o'clock the volunteer fire department reported to Sam that they'd taken in over five hundred dollars at the coin drops they'd set up at the village limits for the building fund. While Sam was counting the take into his carpetbag, Jim Kinneson heard the first faint rumble of thunder. Off to the west the storm Sir Izaak had forecast the day before was making up. Perley Benson donated ten thirty-by-forty-foot rolls of waterproofed tarpaulin to cover the lumber from the dismantled churches.

Jim and Charlie were staking down a tarp over the safe from the former Congo study when Perley and George Quinn sidled up to them.

George cleared his throat. "We just thought it might be best if you fellas were the ones to tell Sam," he said. "Since you seem to have befriended him and all."

"Tell him what?" Jim said, but the question wasn't out of his mouth before he knew and so did Charlie.

"You're going to stiff him, aren't you?" Jim said. "You aren't going to offer him the minister's job. You aren't going to offer him anything."

"We don't have any choice," Perley said. "He isn't ordained.

He talks like a darky, looks a little like one, too. Very likely he's living in sin with that woman he calls his sister. He just isn't, well, damn it all, he isn't one of us."

It was the first time either of the brothers had ever heard Deacon Perley Benson swear.

"And we aren't going to stiff him," George Quinn said. "We're going to pay him for helping us get this far with the new church."

"We're prepared to pay him a thousand dollars," Perley chimed in. "I call that pretty good money for a fly-by-night tent preacher."

"I've got a better idea," Charlie said. "Why don't you just offer him thirty dollars? In silver."

Another clap of thunder, much louder this time. The storm was closing in on the village. Elder George Quinn jumped, whether from the nearby lightning or Charlie's retort was impossible to say. Perley shrugged. "We'll tell him ourselves in the morning," he said. "Time to seek cover, boys. Old Izaak was right. We're about to have us a sockdolager."

Everyone was scattering for shelter. Sam and Glory hurried up the sidewalk in front of the brick shopping block, Sam carrying the carpetbag laden with change and bills from the coin drop. The couple ducked into the bank to make their deposit. Jim held out his hand. A few raindrops spattered off his palm. Up the street Sam and Glory emerged from the bank and cut across the short north end of the green toward the parsonage. The carpetbag swung at Sam's side as they sailed along hand in hand, the wind now at their back.

Charlie began to laugh. "Jimmy," he said. "Did you just see what I saw?"

Jim was still fuming over the church fathers' decision not to hire Sam. "What did you see?"

"I think I saw a bank withdrawal," Charlie said. "And I think we just saw the last of Good Sam and Gloryanne Merryton."

This time there was no discernible interval between the lightning and the crash of thunder. Then Jim was laughing, too, laughing and high-fiving his brother as the sky over the village of Kingdom Common opened up with biblical fury.

The following evening Editor Jim Kinneson and his brother Judge Charlie Kinneson stood on the riverbank above the church pool, stringing up their fly rods. The river was still slightly colored from yesterday's thunderstorm, though falling fast now, and clarifying. Long ago the brothers' father, Editor Charles Kinneson, had taught them that falling water was good fishing water.

"He taught us a lot," Jim said. "Dad."

"He and Mom taught us everything," Charlie said in a rare unironical moment. "Except how to tell the future. What I still can't figure out is why they skipped town in the middle of the night. If they didn't clean out the fund."

Jim opened his fly book and studied the multicolored feathered creations. The book and many of the flies had belonged to their father. Charlie reached over his shoulder and tapped an Adams like the one the big brown trout had hit.

"You think he'll be back?" Jim said.

"Sam? Not a chance."

"Not Sam. That trophy brown."

Charlie shrugged. "I'm not going to make any more predictions," he said. Then his eyes narrowed. He was looking at the tarpaulin over the safe from the former Congo church. Two corners had been pulled loose, Jim assumed by the wind accompanying the storm the evening before, but instead of staking them down again Charlie removed the canvas covering altogether. The heavy door stood open and except for a single scrap of paper the safe was empty. "Luke 2:7," Sam had written in his block lettering on the back of the deposit slip from the proceeds of the coin drop the day before. "'Because there was no room for them in the inn.'"

"Jesus," Jim said. "He had us from the start, didn't he?"

"Every last one of us," Charlie said. "Including you and me. Hook, line, and sinker."

"Well, hell. What should we do?"

"Same thing Sam would do," Charlie said. "Go fishing for that big brown trout. Tell you what, bub. You hook him, I'll land him for you."

4

Sisters

Auction Day in Lost Nation Hollow dawned cloudless. The sky was a deep Canadian blue, though a few wispy shreds of fog crept up the mountainside above the river. The sisters' father, Swale Kinneson, had loved to pronounce that mist climbing up the mountain betokened a fair day ahead. Swale Kinneson had a saying for every weather event. If, after two days of rain, the wind began to shift around to the north, that too indicated fair weather in the offing, a good time to make hay. Unfortunately, Swale was allergic to hay dust. He was also allergic to cows, pigs, chickens, silage, tractor exhaust—and therefore tractors—and, in Miss Madge's opinion, to work. What summer mist and a drying north wind actually meant was a good day for Miss Madge Kinneson and her schoolteacher sister, Miss Mary Mae Kinneson, to make hay. Swale had assured the girls that hay dust would do for him if he set foot inside the barn. " 'Consider the lilies of the field,' " he intoned. " 'They do not toil, neither do they spin.' "

When the hale old man died of natural causes in his ninth decade, the sisters planted him in the family plot above the
homeplace. They commissioned a granite marker, shot
through with flecks of pink quartz that sparkled in the mild
northern sunshine, into which, in accordance with Madge's instructions, the stonecutter had chiseled Swale's name and
dates and the epitaph HE DID NOT TOIL OR SPIN. Mary Mae
had been mortified. Mary Mae had been mortified by nearly
everything Madge had done over the years. She believed that,
long ago, Madge had needed to be taken in hand, like the three
generations of scholars Mary Mae had taught at the Lost Nation schoolhouse. Madge, for her part, believed there was
nothing wrong with her proper elder sister—there was a
year's difference between them, a year Miss Mary set great
store by—that fifteen minutes in the candlelit company of a
man's man, over a bottle of wine, would not rectify.

"Too late for that now," Mr. Frenchy LaMott said to Madge
as they stood in the sisters', now Madge's, kitchen, watching the
sun come up over the Quebec mountains off to the northeast.

Mr. Frenchy LaMott ran the commission sales auction barn
in the Common. He and Miss Madge Kinneson had been
keeping company for twenty years, since Madge's third
husband had gone out to the milking parlor to broom down
the cobwebs and never been seen or heard from in Kingdom
County again. All three of Madge's husbands had been worth-
less. As she frequently reminded Mr. Frenchy LaMott, she
had traded downhill each time she remarried. In the dooryard
of the homeplace there grew an ancient and lovely maple tree
known to the sisters as the marriage tree because Kinneson
women had been married under its boughs for several

generations. Up and down the hollow it was said that the marriage maple in the Kinneson place dooryard brought, to a mat-
rimonial union, the sweetness of fancy-grade maple syrup, the
strength of seasoned timber, and the accommodating give
of a strong and stately tree in a howling line storm. None of
these benefactions seemed to have taken effect in Madge's
three yoke-ups. Husband Number One had been a serial chaser
and card sharp. He'd been shot by an aggrieved husband
during a game of Texas Hold'em in the barroom of the Common Hotel, where at the time Madge had been working as a
waitress. Number Two had inherited Swale Kinneson's porch
glider, out of which, drunk on blackberry brandy, he'd tum-
bled and broken his neck. Madge had buried him next to
Swale with a marker adorned by his name and the word
DITTO. Good-for-Nothing Number Three, Madge claimed,
was still sweeping the cobwebs out of the milking-parlor windows though she would not have guessed that it would take
him this long to complete the task. In the two decades since
his disappearance, she and her close companion Mr. Frenchy
LaMott had never mentioned marriage. As Madge frequently
declared, she was married out. "Three times and out, Mr.
LaMott," she said. Mr. Frenchy LaMott, for his part, had been
in love with Miss Madge since the day, forty-some years ago,
he'd seen her throw a drunk up the three steps leading from
the barroom to the hotel lobby. It was the first time he'd ever
seen a big man thrown up a flight of stairs, and he was
smitten.

Later today, while Madge tended to Miss Mary Mae's final
remains, Mr. Frenchy LaMott, in accordance with Mary's
wishes, would auction off most of Mary's possessions from the

homeplace. All but the cherry breakfront containing Miss Mary's particular friends, a complete set of the Harvard Classics. The breakfront and friends, as well as her half-interest in the house, Mary had left to Madge, along with written instructions for the disposition of her remains. The remains reposed in a Hellmann's mayonnaise jar in the breakfront next to Henry David Thoreau's *Walden*. The proceeds from the auction were to be bequeathed to the Henry David Thoreau Society in Concord, Massachusetts.

The mist off the Lost Nation Branch of the Upper Kingdom River had dissipated. Looking out the south window of the kitchen, Madge half expected to see her schoolteacher sister coming up the lane with half a dozen pan-sized trout on a forked alder stick, fresh-caught for breakfast. Mary had been a neat hand with a bamboo pole and an angleworm. Like her friend Henry David Thoreau.

"You want this sieve to go, Madge?"

"It isn't a sieve, it's a colander. Yes, I want it to go."

"I expect some downcountry dealer would offer a cool thousand for that breakfront. I know a fella runs a dented-in tin-can store with a line of secondhanded paperbacks would probably take those old books off your hands."

"The breakfront and books stay."

"There's a chip on the handle of this sugar bowl."

"I know about the chip on the handle. Get what you can for it. It's a gravy boat, not a sugar bowl."

Miss Mary Mae's cat No Ears, a mammoth orange tom with a head as large as a cauliflower, came slinking into the kitchen and stretched out on the floor in front of the cold Home Comfort range. The tom rolled over onto his back and began working his front paws in the air and purring. No Ears had accompanied Sister Mary Mae down the hollow every school day and suffered the little girl scholars to dress him up in dolly clothes. The boys coaxed him into chasing a button on a string. No Ears and Miss Mary Mae had been inseparable, though in the way of most cats, he did not seem to miss her now that she was gone. Madge did not care for cats.

Mr. Frenchy LaMott looked at No Ears, unsheathing his front claws and retracting them in time to his purring. "I could put that customer to work," Frenchy said. "Keeping down the rats at the commission barn. What would you take for him?"

"Nothing. He belongs here on the place."

"I thought you didn't like cats."

"I don't."

"I'll give you fifty dollars for him."

"You'd soon give me a hundred to take him back."

Frenchy shrugged. "What's this, a scales? Is it an antique? What's it worth?"

"It's a steelyard, for the love of Pete. I have no idea what it's worth. It's worth whatever you can get for it."

"I haven't said a thing right since I arrived this morning," Mr. Frenchy LaMott said to No Ears, now basking on the windowsill in the early sunlight.

Madge pretended not to hear. She was looking at the Currier and Ives reproduction over the kitchen counter: GOOD COUNTRY LIVING. It depicted a winter country scene, probably Christmas morning, with horse-drawn sleighs arriving in the snowy dooryard of a handsome light-yellow farmhouse. Madge had little use for Currier and Ives. Why didn't they show the same dooryard at hog-killing time when you could hear the doomed pigs screaming in terror all the way down the hollow to Miss Mary Mae's former schoolhouse? Or during the diphtheria epidemic that had killed seven of the sisters' great-aunts and uncles, some still not out of their cradles? The front door had been marked in black paint with a foot-high "Q" and nailed shut. Neighbors passed covered dishes in through the same bay window the bodies of the small aunts and uncles were passed out of. Why hadn't Currier and Ives commissioned a scene in which Mary Mae, having dragged their drunken father home from the Common Hotel on a hand-drawn sledge, came upon the hired man about to have his way with eleven-year-old Madge and brained him with a bed warmer? Or Swale butchering Madge's starving riding pony because it was all they had left to eat during the interminable winter of '48? Madge, and Mary Mae too, when she'd been among the quick, could have told Mr. Currier and Mr. Ives a thing or two about good country living.

"I've got a catalogue out in the rig that tells how much those old prints are fetching these days," Mr. Frenchy LaMott said. "We'll get top dollar for it."

"I'm sure the Henry David Thoreau Society will be grateful," Madge said.

"You're getting her half of the house, right?"

"Such as it is."

"Some rich downcountry lawyer'd pay a pretty penny for a house with this view."

"What was it my father used to say? 'You can't eat the view.' The cat and the breakfront and Mary Mae's friends had all better be here when I get back."

Miss Madge got her red-and-green-checked Johnson wool hunting jacket from the peg behind the woodshed door and

handed the jar with Mary Mae inside to Frenchy while she
shrugged into the jacket.

"You take care now, Madge. I'm not sure what you're fixing
to do down there is strictly legal."

"Let me worry about that, Mr. LaMott."

"I wish you'd wait until tomorrow and let me drive you."

"This is between Sis and me, thank you kindly."

Miss Madge set the Hellmann's jar beside her on the bench
seat of the '43 International farm truck and pressed the foot
starter on the floor. It didn't catch.

"Let up and try again," Frenchy called. Madge let up on the
starter. After a few seconds she pressed down on the starter
again. This time the truck came to life. Madge waved out the
window without glancing back, pulled out of the dooryard, and
here, heading up the lane from the plank bridge over the brook,
came an SUV towing a trailer. The first auction-goer of the
day, three hours early to have a good look at the items for sale.
Out-of-state plates, Connecticut Madge thought. A middle-
aged couple, dealers no doubt. The car stopped and the driver
waved Madge down. "We're looking for the Kinneson auction,"
the man said. "The signs seemed to be pointing this way."

"Jesus," the woman said. "Ask her if this is where they
filmed that chain saw movie."

"House on top of the rise just ahead," Madge said. "Look
out, though. There's a den of timber rattlers under the porch
steps."

"There are rattlesnakes up here?" the man said.

"Just watch where you put your foot," Madge said.

She drove off down the mountainside. A minute later the car
and trailer from Connecticut sped past her, heading south.

Madge smiled to herself. There were no rattlesnakes within a hundred miles of Kingdom County.

WALDEN NORTH. Madge could just make out the faded words hand-painted on the cockeyed arrow-shaped sign at the foot of the hill. Madge had been tempted to take it home and use it for kindling a hundred times over the years. The arrow pointed off down an overgrown trace toward the sisters' cedar woods along the river where the hippies had squatted years ago. They'd appeared out of nowhere one September morning in a van as bright as the fall foliage. They referred to themselves as Citizens of the Earth. Sister Mary Mae had taken them in hand. She would, she told Madge, "verse them in country things" or know the reason why. Mary Mae insisted that the hippies be allowed to build their yurts, domes, and crooked little A-frames in the cedars where Swale Kinneson had maintained his whiskey still. Soon Walden North resembled nothing so much as a photograph Madge had seen in a *National Geographic* magazine of a landfill on the outskirts of New Delhi. The hippies were full of enterprises, none of which required much work. To the delight of the local foxes, fisher-cats, and Cooper's hawks, they undertook to raise free-ranging chickens. The women hippies, who did all the work that got done, raised potatoes and reaped potato bugs. One of them claimed to be a potter. Her consort went to keeping bees but raided all the honey to make mead for the holidays and the bees starved to death. One of the Earth Citizens enrolled in a correspondence course in wainwrighting.

The hippies revered Henry David Thoreau though it was unclear to Madge whether any of them had ever read him. They

set out to beautify the roadside ditches of the Kingdom by sow-
ing, hither and yon, the seeds of purple loosestrife, the most
aggressive non-native nuisance plant in the Northeast, which
soon overran every marshy wetland in the county. Swale Kinneson and at least two of Madge's husbands would have contrived a way to get hold of their food stamps and welfare checks
immediately, but Mary Mae cleaned up and deloused and
wormed with tansy tea their otherwise indestructibly healthy
children and enrolled them in the Lost Nation School. Mary
told Madge that the hippies were perpetuating the American
dream and the Vermont tradition of independent-mindedness.
Madge replied that they were perpetuating shiftlessness raised
to a virtue, in the tradition of Swale Kinneson and Henry David
Thoreau. Madge said that there was a reason why Kingdom
County farmers had abandoned their land in the first place and
anyone foolish enough to want to go back to it without the faint-
est notion of how to raise a parsnip deserved whatever the
stony soil and interminable winters dealt out. Against all her
better judgment, Madge gave the hippies rides to town and
back and doctored their frostbitten fingers and supplied them
with groceries when, at the end of each month, they ran out.
On the fifth or sixth summer after they had descended on the
sisters like an Egyptian plague Madge had discovered, growing in a clearing on the mountainside above the homeplace,
several hundred hardy marijuana plants. Not wishing to
lose the farm to the Alcohol, Tobacco, and Firearms bureau,
she had promptly ordered the Citizens off the premises. A
hippie sea-lawyer who had briefly attended a paralegal program presented the sisters with a document claiming that,
after dwelling on disused farmland for three years, and putting

it back into agricultural use, the occupiers could claim title to the property in question. Madge and Mary Mae's second cousin, Sheriff John "Uncle Johnny" Kinneson, said he would come out to Lost Nation and serve an eviction notice but Madge had already escorted the back-to-the-landers off the place at the point of her deer rifle. They had trooped away through the woods in the general direction of Canada, though Madge very much doubted that Canada would have them.

Just south of Kingdom Common, Madge swung onto the entrance ramp of the interstate. An overloaded logging truck hauling a pup, also overloaded, blasted its air horn and swerved out around her. Another eighteen-wheeler was coming up fast behind her. Abruptly, Madge pulled into the passing lane.

Near Windsor a state trooper pulled Madge over. Madge was surprised to see that it was a long-haired hippie trooper. No, it was not. It was a little-girl officer. She looked like Pippi Long-stocking on the cover the book Miss Mary Mae read to her scholars. Madge produced her license and registration. "You need to move over and drive in the right-hand lane, ma'am," the child officer said. "You need to speed up a bit. There's a mini-mum forty-five-mile-an-hour speed limit on the interstate."

"I was sending a message to the big rigs," Madge said. "One of them nearly side-swiped me."

"What's in the mayonnaise jar?" the trooper asked.

"My sister," Madge said.

"Your sister's in the jar?"

"Dead as a doornail."

Officer Longstocking frowned. Then she grinned. "Just stay in the right-hand lane and don't hold up traffic, Mrs. Kin-neson. I'm sorry about your sister."

"If you want the truth, we didn't always see eye to eye," Madge said, and would have told her more, but the officer was on her way back to the cruiser.

WELCOME TO THE COMMONWEALTH OF MASSACHUSETTS, read the large green sign.

Madge pursed her lips. The Commonwealth of Massachusetts wasn't much, nor had she expected it to be. "You aren't missing a thing," she said to the Hellmann's jar.

The International rolled into Concord in the early afternoon. Just ahead was some kind of infernal circular intersection. There were several entrances and exits, and cars were getting on and off it like ants hastening in and out of an anthill. Madge braked to a stop. Behind her horns blared. *Don't give them an inch*, Miss Mary's voice said from the jar. More horns bleated out. The motorist immediately behind her, a large man in a Red Sox cap, shook his fist. "Go Yankees!" Madge shouted back out the window.

Before Madge knew she was going to do it, she jammed the accelerator to the floor and gunned the farm truck into the circle, fully expecting to hear the rending clash of metal and glass breaking. Somehow she got through without wrecking. What would the hippies have said? *Good karma on you.* "Yes, and good riddance to you," Madge said aloud, remembering, with remorse, their pitiful exodus into the Great North Woods.

Like the Commonwealth of Massachusetts, Walden Pond wasn't anything to write home about. A slight young man in a Boy Scout uniform was giving a tour to a class of fifth-graders. The boys were conducting a rock fight. The teachers and parent chaperones were protesting feebly. Miss Mary Mae would have brought that nonsense to a stop in short order.

"Those boys need to be taken in hand," Madge said to a harried-looking teacher.

"Lady, you don't know the half of it," the teacher said.

A little cabin, scarcely more than a hippie shanty, sat on the slope above the pond. The water didn't look right for trout, no real inlet or outlet.

"Where is he planted?" Madge asked the Eagle Scout. "Our boy?"

"Actually, he's buried over in the village cemetery in the family plot."

"I imagine they were real proud of him," Madge said. "The family."

"Well, he wasn't all that well-known in his own lifetime," the Scout said.

"That I believe," Madge said.

The bad boys were threatening to throw the girls into Walden Pond and the girls were dancing around just out of reach and daring them to try it.

"Children," the guide cried out, "what do you suppose Thoreau meant when he said he came to the woods to live deliberately?"

The children paid no attention to him.

"I think he came here to avoid gainful labor," Madge said.

"Madam, Henry David wrote much of the first draft of *Walden* within scant feet of where we are standing."

"Case closed," Madge said, and headed back to the rig with her sister's ashes.

"Well," she said to the Hellmann's jar, "what do you think

about this place? Does it suit you? The pond? We could slip back in and do it after dark. If you want my opinion, it's not what it's cracked up to be."

He brought it alive in his imagination.

"Then he had his work cut out for him. I don't know about you, Sis, but I've had a bellyful of Walden Pond. I've got a better idea."

There was no need to hurry. Madge left the International in a public parking lot downtown and took Miss Mary Mae on a self-guided walking tour. On a footbridge over a shallow stream from which she would not have cared to drink she met a man, probably a professor, reciting a poem to his wife: " 'By the rude bridge that arched the flood, / Here the embattled farmers stood.' " The woman rolled her eyes at Madge.

"Come up to Vermont and I'll show you some real embattled farmers," Madge said. The woman laughed. Madge accompanied the professor and his wife to the village cemetery. Several tourists were hanging around the scribbler's grave and yes, dear Jesus, the professor produced a copy of *Walden* and began reading aloud. He looked a little like Madge's second husband of the porch-glider mishap. He too had styled himself a writer. Once he had written a letter to Madge enumerating her pros and cons. Under "pros" he had been able to come up with only one item: "Likes animals."

Madge walked back downtown and locked Miss Mary in the rig and found an eatery in an old stage tavern. She wondered if the farmers had forgathered here for a few short ones after

putting the Red Coats to rout at the bridge. If she knew farmers, likely they had.

Outside the tavern it was dusk. In another fifteen minutes it
would be good dark. Of course there was no such thing as a
hardware store in downtown Concord, but Madge figured she
could make do with the short-handled spade and an empty feed
sack from the toolbox behind the cab of the International. She
stashed the shovel and the Hellmann's jar inside the sack and returned to the cemetery with them. It was a clear but moonless
night. Now the trick would be to leave no footprint. The Walden
North crowd had been big for leaving no footprint on the
land nor had they. There was no space for a footprint in the junk
they'd left behind after embarking on their exile to Canada.

Madge spread out the burlap sack and began spading
wedges of grass and soil onto it. She got down about three feet
and decided that was deep enough. She unscrewed the lid of the
Hellmann's jar and made the transfer. Over time Miss Mary
would sift down the rest of the way and commingle with what
little was left of the slacker.

"You folks enjoy yourselves now," Madge said.

She replaced the dirt and fitted the wedges of grass back on
top. She doubted that anyone would suspect that the grave
had been tampered with. A night bird, Mary Mae would have
known what kind, called. Twenty minutes later Madge was
headed home.

She pulled off at the first rest area in Vermont and caught
forty winks on the seat of the rig. In Bellows Falls she stopped
at an all-night diner converted from a railway dining car.

The Common at dawn resembled a ghost town. Soon enough it would be one.

Madge turned off onto the Lost Nation road and headed up the Hollow along the brook. This morning there was no mist. No Ears was stretched out on the porch railing in the early sun. Mr. Frenchy LaMott sat on the top step smoking a cigarette. He lifted his hand and Madge waved back. She shut off the engine and the International ticked into silence.

"A dealer from Burlington offered me twenty-five hundred for the breakfront," Frenchy said. "Three thousand if I'd throw in the storybooks."

"They aren't storybooks, they're classics, and I wouldn't part with them for the world," Madge said. "I'd sooner let the breakfront go than the books. You know I don't countenance smoking on the premises, Mr. LaMott. I'll thank you to put out that cigarette."

Mr. Frenchy LaMott dropped the cigarette on the swept dirt yard and ground it out with his heel. "What do you intend to do with them?" he said. "The classics?"

What a question, Madge thought. Exactly the sort of question a scheming Frenchman would ask. Still, Frenchy'd given her yet another inspiration.

"I'm going to read them," she said, meaning it as much as she'd ever meant anything in her life. "What else do you suppose I'd do with them?"

5

Friendship Indiana

Two Fingers Kinneson lost a game of chicken to a muskrat trap when he was six years old. In exchange for the three digits sheared off by the steel jaws of the Victor number-four, the village conferred upon him his name, TF for short, and it stuck. He and his brother, the City of St. Louis, who'd come into this world at a cool twenty-two pounds and continued that trajectory, were carnival roustabouts and small-time con men. They'd grown up on a run-down Vermont farm, scions of the moonshining, deer-jacking, whiskey-running branch of the ubiquitous Kinnesons of Kingdom County. From their earliest boyhood TF and the City were inseparable. They shot out-of-season deer together, dropped out of third grade together at the ages of twelve and fourteen, and the next summer went larruping off on the northern New England fair circuit with the Suggs Bros. Midway Extravaganza and Menagerie of Human Wonderments.

The boys started out working set-up and take-down. Soon

they were operating kiddie rides, manning the Kewpie-doll booth and hammer-and-bell. It was Two Fingers who came up with the Sonny Boy Fund.

"Wait up, mister. I see this billfold drop out of your pocket at the baseball throw."

The mark's hand shot to his hip pocket, the one Two Fingers had just lifted the wallet from. On the sucker's face, panic, then relief as TF handed it back to him.

That's when Two Fingers would produce the cut-off plastic milk jug with a crumpled one and a few sorry dimes and quarters on the bottom, and give it a sad shake. SONNY BOY FUND, he'd scrawled on the side of the jug with a Magic Marker.

"It's a awful slow way to pay for little Bubba's treatments but—" TF's voice would falter and the hook was set. The Sonny Boy Fund worked about 80 percent of the time.

The City, for his part, was something of a savant. He was mechanically inclined and could repair any ride on the midway. He could run the shell game and guess your age within a year and your weight within a pound. Barked ballyhoo for the girlie show, dealt backjack to the lot lice behind the Suggs Bros. camper after hours. At fifteen he began driving the 18-wheel generator truck that powered the rides from fair to field day to dairy festival, with TF up front in the rig with him to read the road signs.

Out on the highway the brothers came upon many a late-night wreck. Against the express instructions of the Suggs Bros.—in fact there was only one Suggs, who traveled in the camper truck with the three elderly gals from the girlie show—TF and the City usually stopped to offer what assistance they could, which often wasn't much, especially when

alcohol, speed, and teenagers were involved. A year or so later
they might come upon a makeshift roadside memorial at the
site of a crash they'd witnessed the last time through. Fading
white crosses, garlands of plastic flowers from the local Dollar
Tree. Hand-lettered epitaphs on scarred bridge abutments and
trees, like the cardboard placard on the huge sugar maple in the
fork of the "Y" just south of the Kingdom County fairgrounds:
WE WILL ALWAYS LOVE YOU TROY AND BRANDY. THE CLASS
OF '92.

Two Fingers shook his head as he read the sign aloud. "It
ain't much, is it?"

"They deserve better if I do say so," the City replied, brak-
ing for the junction. "Port or starboard?"

"Starboard."

"Okeydokey."

"I misdoubt money would be any object," Two Fingers said.

"I misdoubt it would be."

"Well, then," TF said a minute later, and it was settled.

"Don't count on your jobs being here when you come crawling
back broke two months from now," the Suggs brother said.
"You two jump ship now, you're down the road for good."

"We'll finish out the Vermont circuit," TF said. "We
wouldn't want to leave you short-handed."

The boys, whose word was golden, worked out the season.
They told Suggs so long on the last night of the state fair in
Rutland. They'd been with him for nineteen years. "Crazy
bastards," he said by way of farewell, knowing he'd never be
able to replace them.

The day after parting company with the carnival, the brothers picked up a local penny saver and bought, from a recently widowed octogenarian in Manchester who didn't drive, a twelve-year-old Buick Roadmaster with 28,000 easy miles on the odometer. The City, who now estimated his own weight at between 428 and 429 pounds, removed the springs and installed reinforced struts all around. At a pawn shop in Vergennes they picked up a used CB with a police-band scanner. A Radio Shack in Winooski gave them a discount on a GPS and a magnetic blue light for the Buick's roof.

"I reckon we're as ready as we're going to be," TF said.

Wedged in behind the Roadmaster's steering wheel, with the electronically operated front seat set all the way back, the City nodded. "I reckon we are."

Two Fingers made a gesture like a wagon master giving the signal to start up over Donner's Pass. "Forward, ho," he said, and they power-glided off into the night on the next leg of the road trip that had become their life.

With the scanner, the GPS, and the flashing blue light, the brothers were frequently the first players to arrive at the scene of an accident. Often they reached a wreck even before the ambulance-chasing shysters.

For starters, they'd returned to their stomping grounds in Kingdom County to practice. "I'm not telling you what to do, sir, but word is your boy, young Troy, was the best ballplayer ever to come out of the Academy. What I and my brother here was thinking, we could take and mount a nice orange basketball hoop from the Wal·Mark on that wicked old maple tree.

Light her up with one of them mercury yard lights. Maybe display Troy's uniform top and the prom dress Brandy was wearing that night under glass. . . ."

Of course everyone knew that at the time of the wreck Brandy hadn't been wearing her prom dress, or one stitch else, but that was a technicality.

Bingo. It was as easy as A Apple Pie.

Two Fingers discovered in himself a genuine artistic flair. The City, who'd never said much to anyone but his brother, was a born listener. Together they were unstoppable.

Years slipped by. Almost despite themselves, the boys' con slipped into something like legitimacy. When a 747 en route from Paris to New York crashed into a blossoming apple orchard near Brattleboro, killing everyone aboard, the brothers raised a million dollars for their pièce de resistance: a memorial wall of white Vermont marble inscribed with the name of each casualty.

They upgraded from Rodeways and Motel Sixes to Comfort Inns and Best Westerns. Downtime, in the late afternoons and early evenings, they watched their favorite movies. Buddy flicks mainly, *Lonesome Dove*, *The Wild Bunch*, *Road House* with Patrick Swayze and Sam Elliott. When the Roadmaster's odometer turned over for the fourth time, they replaced it with a Coupe de Ville right off the assembly line and as red as a Green Mountain sunset.

Now in their late forties, the boys began to take a few working vacations. They spent the better part of a morning at the Wax Museum of the Criminally Insane at Niagara Falls.

Lollygagged through Wall Drug, gawked at the fragments of alien spacecrafts in Roswell. They joked about the names of certain towns they passed through. Bird-in-Hand and Intercourse.

"Hit your brake pedal, brother mine!" Two Fingers had almost missed the sign, hanging by a nail from a lone fence-post at a forsaken country crossroads: FRIENDSHIP, INDIANA. Into the de Ville's trunk it went, on permanent loan from Hoosier Country.

Not that everything was sweetness and light between them. Like an old married couple who'd been through it all together, the brothers looked the other way a lot. And they never did see eye to eye on health care. Two Fingers ran to the local clinics and ER's on the slightest pretext. The City, on the other hand, didn't hold with doctoring. "You commence to doctor, brother, next you know they sock you in the hospital. People die in hospitals."

"They die at home, too," TF said. "Especially when they refuse to go to the doctor."

Still, both brothers were shocked when Two Fingers's PSA count on his annual blood work at the clinic in Kingdom Common came back through the roof, up 20 points from a safe 1.6 the year before. The local doc shipped him to Hanover for a biopsy and Hanover gave him three months at the outside.

"There," TF said, as though he'd prophesied that this or worse was bound to happen. "I guess we'd best pay a call on Cousin Charles."

By the time the documents had been drawn up, signed, and notarized, it was getting on evening. The boys invited their cousins, Attorney Charlie Kinneson and Editor Jim Kinneson, to dinner at the Common Hotel. Over steak sandwiches they finalized a few details. Then the City and TF headed south out of town, with no fixed destination. The City said he was beat, so TF drove.

"Always something to take the joy out of living, brother," Two Fingers said as they passed the dark fairgrounds.

The City didn't reply immediately. In fact, he didn't reply at all.

TF knew even before he reached over and placed his first two fingers on his brother's massive neck and got nothing.

"Port or starboard?" Two Fingers said anyway as the silhouette of the big sugar maple in the fork of the "Y" came into relief in the headlights.

"Okeydokey." TF goosed the Caddy into overdrive and locked in on the maple. "Good riding with you," he told his brother a split second before impact.

The backhoe cost Charlie and Jim $110 an hour for three hours' work. The flatbed wrecker set them back another two-fifty. They could have charged the boys' estate, but they decided that every penny of that should go to Hanover, as the City and Two Fingers had stipulated.

The hoe hit solid ledge three times before it scooped out a hole large enough to accommodate the Caddy and its occupants. Charlie nailed the plank sign to a cedar post, which he drove deep into the raw blue clay with the splitting mall he'd brought along for that purpose. In accordance with Two Fingers's will, he read aloud the first page of *Lonesome Dove*.

It was early September. The leaves had just started to turn. The sunlight had mellowed over the past month and a cidery scent hung in the amber-tinted air.

"Season's changing," Charlie said to break the silence as he and his brother started back down the mountainside together. "Everything changes."

"Not quite," Jim said, nodding back at the sign on the post.

FRIENDSHIP, INDIANA, it still said in faded dark letters. Then, in fresh paint just below, 'POP. 2.'

6

Kingdom of Heaven

Sheriff John "Uncle Johnny" Kinneson sat in his office on the ground floor of the courthouse studying his recently purchased *Rand McNally Road Atlas*. He had just finished tracing out, with three different-colored Magic Markers, three feasible escape routes from Kingdom Common to Skagway, Alaska. Later that year the sheriff would turn seventy-five. That was the day he'd appointed to load his hunting and fishing gear in the built-in toolbox in the bed of his pickup and hit for the Land of the Midnight Sun. A trim, quiet-spoken man, slight of build, with calm gray eyes and white hair parted neatly in the middle, who shaved twice daily and showered and put on a fresh dress shirt and a suit and tie and buffed his dress shoes seven days a week except when he was going fishing, Johnny'd been enamored with Alaska ever since, as an eighth-grader at the Kingdom Common Academy, he'd memorized "The Cremation of Sam McGee," and promised himself that someday he'd go there.

A lifelong bachelor, Uncle Johnny had long since reached the age when he could have retired on his monthly sheriff's pension and Social Security check. His needs were modest. He was in excellent health and still as good in the woods as any man in the Kingdom. There was just one problem. Although Johnny had not officially run for reelection in more than a decade, the voters of Kingdom County kept writing him in for the job by an overwhelming margin. This year would be different. This year he would steal a march on the electorate. Come Johnny's birthday in late September, he'd make a break for it and never look back. See if he didn't, with the Rand McNally open on the seat beside him, colorful as the fall foliage he was leaving behind.

"Shave-and-a-haircut, two bits." Someone was tapping on the frosted glass of the open office door. There stood Cousin Bear Kinneson in his pink-and-blue flowered housedress and size fourteen square-toed brogans. "Morning, deer," Bear said to the twelve-point buck's head mounted on the wall behind Johnny's desk. Below it was the five-pound brook trout Johnny'd caught in Pond Number Three up by the Canadian border. "Morning, trout," Bear greeted the trophy fish. Then, as if just noticing John, "Morning, shurf."

"Bear," Johnny said. "How many times have I requested that you not call me that?"

Bear clapped his hand, big as a catcher's mitt, to his forehead. "Sorry, shurf. It's just that I can't say sheriff. If I could, I wouldn't say shurf."

"You just did," Johnny said. "Say sheriff."

Bear's eyes, dark as a bruin's, danced with merriment. Nothing delighted him more than the paradoxes of his own nature.

Though he had no feminine mannerisms—Hattie Kittredge, his longtime lady friend and accompanist on the piano when he played out at local dances, could and frequently did testify that Bear "weren't no woman"—he had worn flowered housedresses that he bought off the rack at Benson's Dry Goods forever. A fixture in the village for decades, he had no fixed residence. Sometimes Johnny let him stay overnight as a guest of the county in an empty jail cell. Or he might hole up for a week or two in someone's hunting camp, always leaving the floor swept, the woodbox full, the privy limed.

Most interesting of all, though he couldn't read a note of music, Bear was a musical savant, who could pick up any instrument and play it by ear. He was a three-time North American Old-Time Fiddling Champion. To keep himself in White Owl Cigars, which he smoked two at a time, he played out at Kingdom roadhouses and social functions. Also Bear tuned pianos, sometimes quartering himself in the parlors or guest bedrooms of a customer for weeks on end. Once he spent an entire winter with Editor Jim and Dr. Frannie Kinneson, neither of whom could say no to anyone. In the summertime he played his violin for the town band, which performed on the village green on Thursday evenings and Sunday afternoons.

Other than his modest wardrobe of housedresses, Bear's handmade violin was his single worldly possession. He'd fashioned it himself from native woods. Its sounding board was sugar maple with beautiful oval bird's eyes speckling the grain from a tree Bear had cut himself in the full of the moon in January and seasoned in the open air for a year. The music it brought forth was as sweet as first-run maple syrup. The neck was local white pine, and when Bear played "Your Cheatin'

Heart" and "The Lovesick Blues," crooning along in his gravely voice in perfect pitch, you'd swear you could hear the zephyrs in the lofty tops of the original pine forest singing backup for him. He'd worked from no pattern, borrowing tools from a local cabinetmaker, reinventing an instrument invented six hundred years ago. Bear had never made another violin or would again.

"We going to ride the roads today, shurf?" Bear said. "I and you?"

Johnny sighed. "I do not 'ride the roads,' cousin. Drunks who swill beer out of quart bottles in paper bags between their legs ride the roads. I do perimeter checks. To answer your question, yes. We may do a little reconnaissance work later this forenoon. I thought we might have a bite of breakfast over at the hotel first."

Bear frowned like a magistrate deliberating over an important decision from the bench. "I could go for a bite of breakfast," he said. His eyes danced. His cousin the sheriff always bought him breakfast at the hotel after he'd spent a night at the jail. Often Uncle Johnny underwrote Bear's prodigious lunches and suppers as well.

The sheriff's phone rang. It was Cousin Orwell Kinneson from Lost Nation Hollow, for Bear. After a minute Bear said, "Alrighty, Cousin. Can do. I imagine Uncle Johnny will run me out after breakfast." Orwell said something. "Alrighty, I won't call you cousin, Cousin."

Bear handed the phone back to Johnny to hang up. "He wants me to come out to the Nation and tune an old schoolhouse piano, shurf. And not call him cousin. You believe in the kingdom of heaven, do you, Johnny?"

Bear flashed the sheriff a conspiratorial grin. No one rel-
ished the savant's non sequiturs more than he did himself.

"I'll tell you when I get to Skagway," Johnny said. "How
about you, Bear? You believe in heaven?"

"Yes sir, shurf. When Hattie and I are taking the house on
home with 'The Orange Blossom Special' at the end of the evening, or maybe 'Oh, Them Golden Slippers,' and they're clap-
ping and stomping so the building shakes, you bet I believe in
heaven. Right in the here and now in Kingdom County."

Uncle Johnny had no idea where the kingdom of heaven
might be, assuming that such an entity existed at all. He was
reasonably sure of this much. Wherever it was located, it was
nowhere within hailing distance of the wild northeastern
corner of Vermont where he had been elected to enforce some
semblance of law and order for the last fifty years.

Orwell Kinneson was the tightest man in Kingdom County.
His wife, Eula, a hard-bitten countrywoman in her own right,
boasted that when it came to driving a bargain, there was no
give to Orwell at all. In the early 1950s he'd inherited the family
farm from his parents: a ramshackle house and barn, 160 steep
and stony acres, a couple dozen black-and-white milkers. Fortunately for Orwell and Mrs. Orwell, as the farmer's wife was
generally referred to, the place was unencumbered by a mortgage. In a serious sit-down talk shortly after they were pro-
nounced man and wife, Orwell gave Mrs. O to understand
that the trick to keeping their heads above water was to avoid
all debt whatsoever. Neither a borrower nor a lender be, the miser told his wife with a searching look at her face as if he were

trying to detect in it a latent tendency toward generosity that he'd missed during their courtship. Orville needn't have worried. In this respect he was preaching to the choir. As he would presently discover, Mrs. Orwell was as stingy as he was.

Even so it was widely held in the omniscient Common that it was Mrs. O's idea to lend just enough to their struggling neighbors to enable them to keep their farms afloat for a few more years. When inevitably their places went under anyway, Orwell swooped down like a chicken hawk and scooped them up for back taxes. Soon the couple owned most of the Hollow from the covered bridge just off the county road all the way north to the Canadian border.

In the early 1960s Orwell was the first farmer in the Kingdom to erect a blue Harvestore silo. The loafers in the Common, the feed store hangers-on, and the gang of quasi-vigilantes known as the Green Mountain Boys who, in warm weather, armed with their deer rifles, camped out on the Canadian border in folding chairs and protected the Kingdom against stray day-hikers wandering over the line from Quebec, told Cousin Bear that Orwell's soaring Harvestore was a missile silo. In it was a nuclear weapon to defend the Kingdom from outsiders. Cousin Bear nodded gravely. Then he crinkled up his small, black eyes and exchanged significant glances with Uncle Johnny, making fun of the ne'er-do-wells while they made fun of him.

When, in the '70s, Orwell switched from buckets to gravity-flow pipeline in his maple sugar orchard, many of the Commoners who drove out to his place to buy syrup each spring didn't know what the fluorescent-green tubing strung from tree to tree was for. In the '90s he bought a massive hay baler that spit out quarter-ton bales shrink-wrapped in white plastic. Wheat did poorly in the boreal mountains of northeastern Vermont. Therefore, in addition to hay and corn, Orwell raised buckwheat and rye, thus eliminating the huge grain bills of most Kingdom farmers. His personal habits were irreproachable. He claimed never to have taken a drink or smoked a cigarette in his life. Six feet tall and built like the wrestlers Mrs. O loved to watch on *Monday Night SmackDown,* Orwell was as strong as an ox. By the turn of the millennium he was milking one thousand Holsteins and referring to his farm as an agribusiness. In 2012 he installed the first robotic milking system in the Kingdom. When it came to his farm, the best was good enough and he paid for it, as he never tired of reminding his debtors, in green cash money.

Self-sufficient and driven though he was, and even with Mrs. O keeping the books, Orwell Kinneson could not do all of the work necessary to keep his agribusiness going himself. What he needed most was good help. Trouble was, with the advent, over the course of his lifetime, first of mechanized, then high-tech, farming, the long-standing Vermont tradition of the cantankerous but indispensable hired man who could tinker a comatose tractor back to life, gentle a calf just separated from its mother, doctor a heifer with mastitis, and elevate nonstop grousing to an art form had nearly disappeared. By the time he installed robots to milk his cows, Orwell had already gone through most of the couple of dozen part-time hired men left in the county. While he claimed that he never asked more of a hand than he expected from himself, he prided himself on extracting work from his help by toiling alongside of them and making them keep up with him. He'd worked half to death any number of hapless day laborers sent out by the unemployment and probation and parole offices in St. Johnsbury and Memphremagog, both of which had stopped making referrals to him. Most of the other megafarms in the Kingdom were importing Mexican workers. Orwell had nothing against Mexicans but, like the Green Mountain Boys from the Common, distrusted on general principles anyone not born in the Kingdom. Recently he'd written a definite letter to *The Monitor* recommending that a high electrified fence be built around the county in order to "keep out anyone not from around here." On a few occasions he'd reluctantly asked his cousin, Bear Kinneson, to help him during haying or maple sugaring. Bear'd declined. The fact was, each of the two Kinneson cousins regarded the other as an embarrassment to the family name.

From his dancehall work and piano tuning, Cousin Bear earned enough to keep himself in White Owl Cigars and housedresses to play out in, violin strings, and candy and, occasionally, cut flowers from the I.G.A. for Hattie. Hattie lived with her ancient mother in an apartment in the brick shopping block over *The Monitor* in the Common and worked out during the day as a housekeeper. She and Bear had kept company since their childhood. She was a cousin of Mrs. Orwell's but Orwell and Mrs. O wouldn't acknowledge her, any more than Orwell acknowledged his cousin Bear. In the Kingdom, failing to assist family members in need was unforgivable. Orwell and Mrs. O couldn't have cared less.

Lately Bear had been saving his pennies from his piano-tuning work and odd jobs to buy Hattie Mae a piano of her own. In an account in the Kingdom Common Bank that Uncle Johnny had helped him open, he'd saved nearly five hundred dollars over the past year. He figured that he was getting close to what a serviceable used instrument would cost.

As for Orwell, recently he'd purchased the disused schoolhouse at the foot of the Fiddler's Elbow in Lost Nation Hollow. Along with the schoolhouse and the acre it sat on, Orwell'd acquired a beat-up old school piano. Would Bear be interested in taking a gander at it? Though he wanted no truck with his cousin the miser, Bear was intrigued by the challenge of resurrecting the old instrument.

On their way across the covered bridge leading up to the Hollow, Bear announced to Uncle Johnny, without looking at the speedometer, that Johnny's patrol truck was traveling between sixteen and seventeen miles an hour and the right rear tire was a millimeter out of round. He could tell from the pitch of the tires on the wooden floor of the bridge. Uncle Johnny glanced at the speedometer. Sixteen miles per hour.

Some years ago Johnny'd introduced Bear to a friend of his, a professor of music theory at Harvard who summered in the Kingdom with his family. The professor had heard Bear play at a box supper. He was so impressed by Bear's repertoire that he invited the savant to visit Cambridge for a few days that fall. One evening they heard the college orchestra play a medley of classical pieces including Brahm's lullaby. After the concert Bear played the entire first chair violin's part back to the director from memory. According to the professor, Bear altered only one bar of the score, in the director's estimation improving it slightly. Upon Bear's return to the Kingdom Johnny asked him how he liked Harvard. The fiddler gave the question some thought, then said he liked it fine and could probably have spent another entire week on campus and still not learned all they had to teach him. Bear laughed and his eyes sparkled. Whether he was poking fun of Harvard or himself or all of the ironies in the history of mankind was impossible to know. Bear had attended, on the campus, a seminar in ancient classical literature. One evening over steak sandwiches and home fries at the Common Hotel he'd repeated the professor's lecture verbatim to Uncle Johnny. "Yes, sir," Johnny'd said when Bear finished.

Just beyond the covered bridge rose School Hill. Partway down the hill the road bent sharply. This was the Fiddler's Elbow. The abandoned schoolhouse sat just above the crook in the elbow. Uncle Johnny dropped Bear off in the overgrown schoolyard, where Orwell was waiting in his red farm truck.

"Mis-sus Kinneson," Orwell greeted Bear. Bear was wearing a plain brown housedress. He stood eye to eye with his cousin and was as broad through his shoulders as an axe handle is long. A heavy two-day beard darkened his jowls. In one hand he held his violin case, in the other a fishing tackle box containing his piano repair tools and materials.

"You still in the piano-tuning racket, are you?" Orwell said.

"They make a racket after I tune them, all right," Bear said.

"School," Orwell said as he stood in the daisies and paintbrush in the yard. "I hated every minute of it."

"You wanted to be out earning money," Bear said.

Orwell grimaced, which was the closest Bear had ever seen his cousin come to smiling. "I reckon," he admitted. It was the one moment of accord he'd had with his cousin, or perhaps with anyone other than Mrs. O, in years.

"My people never put me to school," Bear said. "They was

a-scart the other young'uns would poke fun of me. My mother taught me to read and cipher to home."

Orwell was becoming uncomfortable with the tenor of the conversation. Not for him to confide in, or be confided in by, the village dolt. "Let's get on with this," he said, and shouldered his way through the boys' door.

The schoolhouse had been abandoned for thirty years. Orwell's thought was to slap on a new roof and replace the rotting sills, then fob it off on some out-of-stater for a hunting camp or summer place. As for the piano, it probably hadn't been played for decades. If Bear could get it into any semblance of working order, he knew a dealer in secondhand furniture who'd probably give him a hundred dollars for it.

The entire southeast wall of the school consisted of a large window divided into thirty-two-foot square panes. The glass was layered with dust and lavendered and wavy with time. Bear was surprised that the window hadn't been shot out by local boys or drunken hunters. Then again, there were no families with children remaining in the Hollow, and Orwell had posted the schoolhouse and surrounding fields and woods. Anyone with a grain of sense who knew Orwell would think twice about shooting at his property.

Enough sunlight still fell through the schoolhouse window for Bear to get a good look at the piano. It wasn't promising. An elderly upright Baldwin with several chipped and missing ivories, in need of revarnishing, covered with sparrow droppings, the lid missing, a number of hammers missing their felt striking pads, the sounding board cracked. It looked as though some wild animal, maybe a raccoon, had at some point raised a litter inside the belly of the instrument. Three of the rolling casters were gone. One leg had snapped in two so that the lid-less instrument listed off like a drunkard at the BYOB dancehalls Bear performed in.

"Well?" Orwell said.

Bear supposed that he'd seen sicker pianos. Not many, though. He tried a key. It sounded like a wind-up alarm clock starting to go off, then abruptly stopping. He tapped an upper-register ivory. Nothing. He let his fingers, unbidden, play the opening bar of "I Fall to Pieces." He doubted Patsy Cline could have recognized it. Yet there was something there in the few keys that resounded, something cheery, like Hattie's face when she stood up at the piano like Jerry Lee Lewis to hammer out the chords for "Oh, Them Golden Slippers," and that's when the idea came to him. He would buy the ancient instrument from Orwell as it was, repair it, and present it to Hattie.

The thought of Hattie's happiness made Bear Kinneson happy, but not for long. When he offered Orwell one hundred dollars for the Baldwin as it stood, the wealthy farmer shook his head. "You tune it and repair it," Orwell said. "Then we'll talk."

Bear didn't much care for this arrangement. But if he still wanted the piano for Hattie, as he very much did, he had no choice. Orwell agreed to pay him ten dollars an hour, and to reimburse him for all necessary materials. Apart from his inspiration to present the Baldwin to his longtime girlfriend, Bear was also excited about the opportunity to resurrect what had once been a fine musical instrument. In his tackle box were all of the tools and many of the replacement parts neces-sary to repair an elderly piano: glue, sandpaper, hammer felts, piano wire, chisels, a jigsaw and jigsaw blades, jars of piano varnish and shellac made from the shells of beetles from Sri Lanka. He wrote out a list of supplementary materials for Orwell to phone in to the Baldwin Company in Elmira, N.Y., for next-day delivery in Kingdom County. He borrowed the broom in the back of Orwell's truck, swept out the guts of the piano, wiped it clean of dust and bird leavings with a rag he'd wet in the nearby stream.

Over the next week, working methodically, letting his hands think for him, Cousin Bear Kinneson replaced the missing and chipped ivories on the schoolhouse piano. He restrung the wires, replaced the felt striking heads of the hammers, and fashioned a new pine sounding board. He installed a new foreleg, repainted in gilt letters the BALDWIN CO. on the inside of a replacement lid. He sanded the entire exterior with the finest-grain sandpaper and coated it twice with varnish and shellac. Replaced the rolling casters. Occasionally Orwell dropped by at the schoolhouse to watch him work. He badgered Bear to play a few notes but Bear refused to try out the Baldwin until all of the renovations had been completed.

One afternoon in late August Bear applied the final coat of shellac to the piano. That evening the annual flying-ant hatch began to emerge, with the translucent-winged creatures crawling out of sidewalk cracks, house foundations, rock walls, and boulders along streams and rivers throughout the Kingdom. The next morning Johnny dropped Bear off at the schoolhouse, then stopped at the pull-off beside the covered bridge at the foot of the Fiddler's Elbow to fish the ant hatch on the pool below the bridge. To Bear's surprise, Orwell was waiting for him at the school.

For his test run Bear played a movement from the Brahms

piece he'd heard at Harvard. "Needs breaking in," he said. "But she'll do."

"Fair enough," the farmer said, and handed Bear eight fifty-dollar bills.

Bear reached in his dress pocket for the four hundred and eighty dollars Uncle Johnny'd withdrawn from their special account the day before, but Orwell held up his hand, palm outward, like a traffic policeman. "I'll let her go for two thousand, not a nickel less," he said. "I listed it in yesterday's *Monitor* and had four calls already."

Bear Kinneson had never had two thousand dollars at the same time in his life. "I'll give you the one thousand now and work off the balance on your farm. Haying, mending fence, putting up winter wood. Whatever."

"Nope," Orwell said. "Cash on the barrelhead or I'll sell her to somebody else this afternoon."

The morning sun came streaming through the many-paned schoolhouse window. Bear knew that Uncle Johnny or Jim or Charlie Kinneson would lend him the additional funds that he needed to buy the piano. They'd give him the money outright. Bear was turning that possibility over in his mind when Orwell made his mistake. He said, "Old Hattie doesn't need any concert-hall state-of-the art Steinberg or whatever. It'd be like putting a chandelier in an outhouse."

Bear seemed not to have heard Orwell's remark. He was down on his hands and knees under the Baldwin. The piano seemed to be levitating. Up it rose, inch by inch, as if bewitched. Orwell realized that Bear was lifting it off the floor. With the quarter-ton piano balanced on his bent back, Bear took a step toward the big window made up of little windows. The piano tipped like a dory in a high sea. Bear took another staggering step. He steadied himself, broke into a stumbling run, and heaved the piano through the schoolhouse window. The explosion of shattering glass was followed instantly by the crash of the piano smashing to flinders in the schoolyard, where it lay in a scarcely recognizable heap, its legs snapped off, its lid smashed to kindle, some of its keys ten feet away in the early-summer paintbrush and daisies.

Bear straightened up, his back crackling. He picked up his tackle box in one hand, his fiddle case in the other, and headed out of the girls' entrance of the schoolhouse and down the hill toward the bridge. Behind him Bear heard Orwell start up the truck. He glanced over his shoulder. The truck was headed his way. Bear continued down the hill into the Fiddler's Elbow at his usual lumbering gait. He'd be damned if he'd give the road to the likes of Orwell Kinneson.

Orwell blasted his horn. The truck bumper smacked into the backs of Bear's thighs. Orwell chivvied him along with the bumper. This was the scene that Uncle Johnny Kinneson beheld from the pool below the covered bridge. At every second or third step the bumper of Orwell's truck clipped Cousin Bear. Johnny started fast up out of the river, reeling in his fly line.

Partway down the Fiddler's Elbow, just below the crook, a stone water bar stretched diagonally across the road. As Bear approached the bar, he looked back over his shoulder again and lost his footing, tripping over the shallow trench. He threw out his hands to break his fall. His tackle box flew off into the roadside puckerbrush and the fiddle case landed on the grassy hummock in the middle of the lane. Bear had to roll out of the way fast to avoid being run over. Johnny came over the bank just in time to see Orwell swerve his left tires onto the hump in the lane. The truck came to a stop. It turned around in the pull-off beside Johnny's patrol truck. Unhurriedly, Orwell headed back up the road toward his showplace atop the hill.

Neither Bear nor Orwell pressed charges against the other though Uncle Johnny urged Bear to do so.

"Orwell is who Orwell is," Bear told Johnny on their way back to the Common. "But you know what Toynbee says, citing old Thucydides. 'The mill of the gods grinds slow but it grinds exceedingly fine.' I learnt that at Harvard."

"Did you now?" Johnny said. "Say what, Bear?"

"Alrighty, shurf? No charges against Orwell? We'll let the mill of the gods do its work?"

Johnny sighed. Seventy-four going on seventy-five years old and what to show for it? A bronze star and Purple Heart from Pork Chop Hill for fending off a mob of Chinamen. A shurf's badge. A friend named Bear.

"No charges," Johnny said.

In the Common, word of the destruction of Cousin Bear Kinneson's violin at the hands of Orwell Kinneson traveled like a forest fire in high wind. Perhaps the sheriff told his kinfolks, Editor Jim Kinneson and Judge Charlie Kinneson, over cold ones at the hotel dining room that evening. Perhaps Bear mentioned it to Old Man Lum Perkins at the bottle redemption room in the back of the I.G.A. By midmorning the incident at the covered bridge was all the talk at the feed store, post office, and courthouse. Some of what was reported was remotely accurate.

In the early afternoon, Bear came shambling into Johnny's office, already talking as he came through the door, something about Harlan Kittredge and Old Man Quick and Parmalee White and the rest of the Green Mountain Boys planning on "paying a call" on Orwell that night. Something Bear'd overheard at the feed store about burning a cross and a little tarring and feathering being in order, the border militia to muster up at the feed store shortly after midnight. "I ain't telling you what to do, shurf, but you'd best get over to the Blue Seal and nip this in the bud. Them boys have started drinking already. There's no telling what they might do come nightfall."

"I can tell you what they're going to do," Johnny said.

"What?"

"Exactly nothing," Johnny said. "Thanks for the tip."

The Green Mountain Boys headed out of the village in a cavalcade of pickups and farm rigs, led by Harlan's lumber truck, horns bleating, lights flashing like an old-time torchlight procession celebrating a baseball championship. They got just as far as the village limits on the county road. Johnny'd parked his white patrol pickup across the road, blue lights rippling. He was standing beside the truck, holding his old Louisville Slugger. The patriots came to a ragged stop. Harlan and two or three others got out and approached the sheriff.

"Yes, sir, gentlemen," Johnny said, his voice light, conversational, pleasant. "You boys can slope on home now, get your beauty rest." He leaned the ball bat against his truck and clapped his hands as if shooing a gaggle of kids off the village green to meet a curfew.

"Now, Uncle Johnny," Harlan said. "These proceedings don't involve you. You know what happened up to the Nation this forenoon. It's all over town, how old Orwell dragged Cousin Bear on a log chain behind his rig from the schoolhouse clean down to the covered bridge. We're just exercising our right to lawful assembly. We're going to have a little talk with Mr. Orwell is all. Time was, he'd have been tarred and feathered at the least."

"Time was," the sheriff said, "when I had a nice natural swing." He picked up the bat and made a couple of half-cuts with it, like a baseball player getting ready to step into the batter's box. "I never was that much of a long-ball hitter. Never did try for the fences. More of a contact man, go with the pitch. As for you boys, I don't want you out riding the roads at night without headlights."

"There's nothing the matter with our head—" Harlan started to say. He jumped back and cursed as Johnny stepped up to his lumber truck, cocked the Louisville Slugger and shattered first one, then the other headlight. Working methodically, the sheriff walked down the line of half a dozen vehicles, smashing out their headlights. Partway along he paused. "Moneyball they call it nowadays. No more bunts, hit-and-run, going the other way for a singleton or two-bagger." Johnny demonstrated his point with a nice inside-out swing, smashing out one, then the other headlight of Old Man Lum Quick's new Ford pickup. Lum Quick let out a howl as if the sheriff had demolished his kneecaps.

"You fellas have enough to do, protecting our borders," Johnny said. "Leave me to handle the sheriffing. That's what they keep electing me to do though I wish they wouldn't. Have a nice rest of the evening now. I'm glad you see the light."

"By God, John, this won't stand," Parmalee White said. "I'm going to talk to Judge Charlie. You can't be taking the law into your own hands."

"Parm, you took the words right out of my mouth." Johnny returned to the patrol truck and slid the bat into the gun rack above the front seat.

"You can kiss that badge goodbye," Old Man Lum Quick said. "You're going down the road, Johnny-boy."

"That's probably the only way I'll ever get to Skagway," Uncle Johnny said. "Goodnight, gentlemen."

The first sign of fall in the Kingdom was a certain subtle mellowness in the late-afternoon sunlight on a clear day in mid-August. You knew it when you saw it. Then came the Kingdom Fair. Orwell's Holsteins won Best Herd in Show for the fifth consecutive year. Accepting the blue ribbon in his dairyman whites and boat-shaped white paper cap, Orwell looked even grimmer than usual.

Soon after Labor Day the few remaining farmers along the county road and out in the hollows could be seen cutting fir and spruce brush to bank the foundations of their farmhouses against the seven-month Kingdom winters. The weathered houses looked encircled by great holiday wreaths. Flock after flock of Canada and snow geese went over, tracing the Appalachian mountain chain south from Quebec to Georgia. In the Kingdom, where spring is heartbreakingly late, brutally short, and often scarcely distinguishable from winter, fall is the season of beginnings and anticipation. With autumn came apple picking and cider making, corn cutting, fall foliage time when the hills and mountainsides were aflame with reds, purples, yellows, oranges. Sometimes farmers eked out a third cutting of hay, known as the quill, short but rich in nutrients. Marsh hawks floated low over the freshly cut fields in search of mice and voles. Monarch butterflies stopped at high mowings to sip nectar from fall clover before sailing on to Mexico. Brook trout assumed their tropically colored spawning attire. The Red Sox, as beloved in the Kingdom as in Boston, did or did not make the playoffs.

One morning in mid-October, a few days after the peak of foliage season, Orwell Kinneson went out to his milking parlor at 5:45. Now that robots did most of his milking, he could get an extra hour of sleep in the morning. Away to the east, behind the northern Presidential Range of the White Mountains, a strip of peach-tinted sky hinted at the impending dawn. Soon the mountains would be snowcapped.

When Orwell did not return to the house at 8:00 for his usual farmer's breakfast of ham or steak and eggs, home fries, oven-baked bread with homemade strawberry preserves, coffee hot and black by the mugful, Mrs. O went to the kitchen window and peered out. The barn lights still appeared to be on though it was unlike Orwell to waste electricity. By 8:30 her husband had still not appeared. Mrs. Orwell put on the rubber boots she wore to gather eggs and work in her garden on dewy mornings and slogged across the barnyard to the dairy. She was relieved not to find the farmer sprawled out on the cement floor of the milking parlor, a victim of a heart attack, which to this day is the fate of so many Kingdom farmers, from the physical and mental wear and tear of their incessant work. But where had he gone? His farm truck was in the three-sided machinery shed where he usually parked it. "Taken up." The expression leaped into Mrs. O's mind from a *Twilight Zone* re-run she'd seen recently in which an entire New England village not unlike the village of Kingdom Common had been carried off by aliens. It occurred to Mrs. O, with a small guilty thrill, that if in fact Orwell had been taken up, and the extra-terrestrials decided, for the sake of science, to put up with him for a time, she might yet make it to Orange City, Florida, where her sister owned several condos. In the meantime she returned to the house where, for the first time in her life, she called a neighbor to ask for help.

Other than Orwell, Ben Currier III was the last farmer left in Lost Nation Hollow. He had no intention of selling out, and thus Orwell had not spoken to him for many years. He responded to Mrs. O's request for assistance immediately. While Ben finished milking Orwell's herd, Mrs. Orwell searched the rest of the barn and the outbuildings. Nothing. "I'm not telling you what to do, Eula," Ben finally said. "But I guess about now I'd be calling Uncle Johnny."

Hastening out the county road up into the hills east of the village with Cousin Bear, Sheriff John Kinneson had the impression that he was traveling from one climate zone to another. In town the maples lining the green were at peak color. Here in the hill country the leaves had faded. Some had already blown away. When the call had come in from Mrs. Orwell,

Johnny'd been on his way out the door for his weekly trip to Pond in the Sky to set up his radar gun for speeders near the local elementary school. In express violation of a recent edict from Montpelier prohibiting law enforcement officials from giving rides to unauthorized passengers, Bear was riding along with him.

"I don't imagine Orwell's gone too far," Johnny said to make conversation.

"I'm sure he hasn't," Bear said. "After that hoo-ha last night where you busted up them Klansmen, he wouldn't want to leave the wife alone up there. Orwell's suing me for the cost of a new Baldwin upright. Nine thousand dollars."

"Sue him back for the cost of a new violin."

"Go to law? That's not our way of doing things up here, shurf. You of all folks know that. I believe that's old Orwell right there, ain't it? Hanging from that beam."

"Jesus H. Christ!" Johnny shouted. He slammed on his brakes and the pickup skidded to a stop just inside the far end of the bridge. Dangling by his neck with his knees drawn up to his chest and his hands tied behind them was the unmistakable bulk of Orwell Kinneson. "Trussed up like a turkey, ain't he, shurf? Look there. He's grinning."

" 'Sufficient unto the day is the evil thereof,' " Johnny said. Four hours later he was headed for Skagway.

John Kinneson hadn't been in Alaska a month when he came across an ad in the paper for a night security guard at the local Walmart. In his second week on the job he foiled a carjacking in the parking lot. The following day he discovered a woman in the early stages of Alzheimer's wandering in the sporting goods department and helped her locate her son. The next week he nabbed two boys shoplifting baseball caps and linked them up with the local Police Athletic Youth Hockey Program. Several months later he landed a job as assistant chief inspector with the Skagway Constabulary Department. He e-mailed Editor Jim Kinneson that compared to maintaining law and order in Kingdom County, policing a frontier town just south of the Yukon River was a walk in the park.

Back in the Kingdom the investigation of Orwell's lynching—the first in the history of Vermont—had sputtered out. As Johnny's young police academy–trained replacement brought in from Montpelier told Jim in an interview for *The Monitor*, the main problem was that none of the evidence matched up. The rope Orwell'd been bound and lynched with seemed to have come from the release pull of the long-disused overhead hayforks in Orwell's barn loft. Wouldn't whoever killed him have brought their own rope? Could he have somehow crawled out on the bridge beam, tied himself up, and dropped to his death in such a way as to suggest that he'd been murdered? Unlikely. The Kingdom County coroner, Dr. Frannie Lafleur Kinneson, reported that Orwell had been struck in the head with a blunt instrument, and that he had died from strangulation or asphyxiation before he'd been strung up, not from a broken neck. The most probable suspects were the Green Mountain Boys, who seemed to have an alibi for the early-morning hours of the day Orwell was killed. They were playing poker at the feed store office. The young sheriff, formerly a decorated state trooper, told the editor he felt like a man trying to assemble a thousand-piece jigsaw puzzle with pieces from a thousand different puzzles.

Presumably, Orwell had been kidnapped before he was killed. In waltzed the F.B.I. The federal prosecutor in Burlington convened a grand jury to determine whether there was enough evidence to bring charges. Uncle Johnny testified by Skype from Skagway for a day and a half. When asked who in the Kingdom might wish Orwell dead, he replied, "Everyone." Mrs. Orwell stuck to her original theory that Orwell had been whisked off in a spaceship. "I imagine he acted up and they dumped him out the back," she told the jury one snowy December morning. They came in with no indictment, ruling Orwell's death a probable suicide. Editor Jim Kinneson congratulated them, in an ironical editorial in *The Monitor*, pointing out that for the first time in the history of the world a suicide had tied himself up in knots that would have stymied Harry Houdini, then lynched himself.

The following spring Hattie Kittredge's mother died and Hattie moved into an assisted-living facility in St. Johnsbury, where Cousin Bear visited her every Thursday and Sunday afternoon. Sometimes they entertained the other residents with a musical interlude, Hattie banging away at an old piano, Bear bowing the violin the Green Mountain Boys bought to replace the magical instrument Orwell ran over with his truck. The new fiddle was perfectly serviceable but everyone agreed that even Bear couldn't coax from it notes as sweet as first-run syrup from a north-slope sugar orchard. Nor, citing liability issues, would the new sheriff allow him to sleep in a jail cell or ride with him in the patrol truck. That summer Mrs. O sold her and

Orwell's vast holdings to a consortium of investors from the Netherlands wishing to conceal unreported earnings in American real estate. The Dutch group hired an extended family of Mexicans to run the farm and Mrs. O moved to Orange City, Florida, and bought a condo from her sister. There she diligently began work on a novel about time travelers from the far reaches of the universe who shanghaied a miserly Vermont farmer. She sent Editor Jim Kinneson her finished manuscript, which Charlie tried to persuade Jim to serialize in *The Monitor*. This Jim declined to do.

Bear didn't play out at dances so much, but one wintry night a year and a half after the lynching, on his way back to the Common from a kitchen junket in Pond in the Sky, he crawled into a dry culvert and froze to death. Jim called Uncle Johnny the next morning with the news.

"Well, I'm sorry, Jimmy," the Skagway constable said. "There was only one Bear."

"We won't see his like again," Jim agreed.

From the Land of the Midnight Sun, where there would be little sun at all for the next two months, came a pause. Then, picking up on the last conversations they'd had before Johnny hit for Skagway, "Then again, Jimmy. What if an uncommonly clever fella made a murder look like a suicide made to look like a murder?"

"Bear," Charlie said when Jim relayed Johnny's speculation.

"Bear," Jim said. "Johnny never really intended to leave the Kingdom. Alaska was his safety valve. He left because he couldn't bear, no pun intended, to arrest Bear."

"Well, good," Charlie said. "Because I sure as hell couldn't bear to sentence him."

Questions remained. What did Orwell's assailant hit him on the head with? No blunt instrument was ever discovered. And hadn't Bear spent that night sleeping in his cell at the courthouse? In the end the murder of Orwell Kinneson remained as mysterious as the source of the savant's musical genius.

That Fourth of July was the first in forty years that Bear would not march up the length of the green with the town band. Jim, standing on the heaved and cracked sidewalk in front of the brick shopping block with Dr. Frannie, Judge Charlie, and Charlie's wife, Athena Allen Kinneson, would miss the sight of him, dressed like a countrywoman of fifty years ago and chewing on two cigars, leading the band up the common playing "Stars and Stripes Forever" on his homemade violin. The passing of Bear Kinneson had left a gap in the life of the village, as if the courthouse or Common Hotel had burned down.

Faint at first, then increasing in volume, the familiar John Philip Sousa piece swelled over the common as, out from behind the United Church across the street from the short south end of the green, came the band, dwindled now to a third of their original number. Each of the dozen or so remaining musicians wore a housedress. Some were smoking one or two cigars. The crowd around the perimeter of the green began to applaud. The band broke into "The Orange Blossom Special" as the onlookers cheered. Jim snapped pictures for the paper. In his mind's eye he saw plainly the enormous visage of Cousin Bear, beaming down from high above the mountaintops at the glorious and horrifying foolishness of his Kingdom of Heaven.

7

Lonely Hearts

"Take a listen to this, Jimmy," Jim's brother Charlie said, rattling that afternoon's edition of the *Memphremagog Daily Express*.

> *Dear Lonely Hearts,*
> *Fun-loving blonde, late twenties, accountant at local firm, seeks gentleman friend 25–35 for companionship, possibly more.*
>
> *Most sincerely,*
> *Tall Drink of Water*

"You ought to check her out, bud," Charlie continued. "That 'possibly more' is intriguing."

"My God, Charlie," Athena Allen Kinneson, Charlie's wife, said: "Jim's what, twenty-seven years old. He's capable of scouting up his own dates. Lonely hearts ads are for desperate people."

Charlie and Athena and Jim were having steak sandwiches and cold ones in the dining room of the Common Hotel. Jim had recently returned to the village from Boston, where he'd been working as a sportswriter for the *Globe*, to write for his father's weekly, the *Kingdom Common Monitor*. Jim and his dad had made a deal. If, after a year, Jim wanted to stay on, his father would make him a partner. Charlie was already a successful local defense attorney. Athena was principal at the regional high school.

"I had all kinds of dates in college," Jim said. "And in Boston. Athena's right. If I want to go out, I can find somebody to go out with."

"I don't know," Charlie said, tearing the lonely hearts ad out of the paper. "Up here in the Kingdom, most girls get married right out of school. You've been home for how long, a month? We'll have to take you up to Ste. Catherine Street and get you back in practice."

Ste. Catherine Street was Montreal's red-light district.

"That is just so vile," Athena said. She patted Jim's hand. "Don't pay any attention to the matchmaker here, Jimmy."

Athena had been Jim's beloved English teacher at the Common Academy, back before the union school was voted in. Sometimes Jim still saw her in that light. She and Charlie had argued since first grade. It was how they communicated with each other.

It was a weeknight, still early in the evening. The two brothers and Principal Athena were the only customers though Jim had the uncomfortable notion that the deer and bear heads mounted on the dining room walls, and even the trophy trout behind the bar, were eavesdropping on their conversation.

Before Jim could change the subject, Charlie said, "Jim's been gun-shy around girls ever since your cousin Frannie went off to college in Canada, Theenie. We need to help him get back in the saddle, so to speak."

"Jesus, Charlie," Jim said though he couldn't help laughing. It was impossible for him to be angry with his brother. For that matter, what Charlie'd said about Jim's high school sweetheart was true. He'd never felt the same way about anyone else. Not even close.

Outside, it was a rare warm night for early April in the Kingdom. Armand St. Onge Jr., the hotel proprietor, had left the front door ajar, and Jim could hear the muted thundering of the High Falls on the river behind the hotel, swollen from snowmelt up in the hollows. Later that month the great rainbow trout that dwelt in the depths of Lake Memphremagog would make their annual spawning run up the river, leaping the High Falls in the Common, their crimson sides glowing like fire. Anglers from all over New England would come to the Kingdom to fish for them though only the Commoners understood the secret of catching them on their own orange eggs sewn up in small squares cut from nylon stockings. Frannie herself had been the best at distinguishing between a bite and the tap-tap-tapping of her sinker bouncing along the gravel bottom of the river and just how much pressure to put on a hooked and leaping trout in the cascading whitewater below the falls.

Fondly, Athena said, "Jim's woolgathering again. Writing in his head."

"Jim's always writing in his head," Charlie said. "That's what writers do. They write."

"Thanks but no thanks, bro," Jim said, standing up. "Tonight's production night, I have to get over to the *Monitor*."

Jim left the letter from Tall Drink of Water on the table. One thing was certain. He had absolutely no intention of responding to this or any other lonely hearts ad in any newspaper. End of story.

Dear Tall Drink of Water,

   I am 27 and live in the village of Kingdom Common. After graduating from the University of Vermont, I worked for The Boston Globe *for five years, the last two covering the Red Sox. Currently, I'm writing for my father's paper, the* Kingdom Common Monitor. *Also, I am partway through a collection of fictional stories about the Kingdom, where I was born and raised. I like to fish for trout, play town-team baseball, and read, and have no objection to 'companionship and possibly more.' Would you consider going out to dinner and the movies with me this Saturday evening?*

Very truly yours,
Jim Kinneson

They met at the Westside Restaurant in Memphremagog, overlooking the bay of the big transborder lake of the same name. Betsy was half a head taller than Jim. She had long elegant legs and long blond hair that appeared to Jim to be natural. Her brown eyes were direct and kind. He liked her immediately.

She began the conversation by saying that she had two small children, a girl and a boy, from an ill-advised teenage marriage. She went on to say that she always had and always would put her son and daughter first. Jim admired both her priorities and her candor. She wore a blue dress embroidered with white and yellow violets, low heels, a practical spring-and-fall jacket. She ordered a ginger ale but didn't bat an eye when Jim asked the waitress for a Bud. It turned out that she had three brothers Jim had played ball against in high school. She had an accounting degree from the local community college and worked as the head bookkeeper at the plywood mill across the bay.

After dinner they walked up the street to see *Horror of Dracula*, a Hammer Film production, which they both found highly amusing. Later, at a local café where they went for coffee, each of them made a disclosure. The sensible and responsible Betsy surprised Jim by confiding that she had inherited certain unusual abilities from a French Canadian great-aunt. As a writer of stories, Jim was equally skeptical of, and fascinated by, the supernatural. He inquired: Could Betsy tell the future? She smiled and shook her head. In her opinion the future didn't yet exist to be told. "But sometimes I can sense things about a person's past," she said.

"What do you sense about me?" Jim asked her.

"I could be wrong," Betsy said. "Have you lost someone, someone you really, really loved?"

A chill ran up Jim's back. Not that nearly everyone hadn't, but still.

"They didn't die," Jim said. "I mean she didn't."

Betsy gave him an encouraging smile. This was an extraordinary young lady, and the next thing he knew Jim was telling her about Frannie, his beautiful high school girlfriend. How they'd competed fiercely for top academic honors, then spent every waking moment outside of school together.

"So what happened?" Betsy said.

"She went off to Canada to go to college. I went to the state university in Burlington."

"Ten years ago," Jim's date said. "That's a long time."

"Tell me about it. To return to the present, this has been a good evening, Betsy. Can we do it again?"

Betsy smiled. She thought for a moment. "Sometimes, Jim, a person doesn't need any special powers to forecast the future. This beautiful gone-away girl? I could never compete with her. For one thing, she'd always stay young in your heart. And what if she came back?"

"She isn't going to."

"But if she did?"

What could Jim say? Nothing. He knew that the good-looking accountant with kind, brown eyes was right.

Betsy rose, slipped into her jacket. Jim drove her to her place across town, and walked her to the door. She put out her hand, then withdrew it, bent down slightly and kissed him on the cheek. "Thank you for the good evening, Jim."

Early the next morning over coffee at the hotel Jim filled in Charlie on his lonely hearts date. "Women know things like that," Charlie said when Jim finished. "We'll try a different approach."

"We'll do no such thing," Jim said. "No more advice to the lovelorn. From now on I'll arrange my own dates, thank you kindly."

"Give me a few days, I'll get back to you," Charlie said.

"Meanwhile, let's hit the bend pool at the foot of Clay Hill to-night. Those spawned-out trout on their way back to the big lake are ravenous at this time of the year."

"No, no, no, and no," Jim said to his brother a few evenings later. He lifted his hands palms outward, as if to ward off all further suggestions. The Kingdom Common Outlaws had just finished their first baseball practice of the year. In the early-spring dusk Jim and Charlie were sitting on the third-base bleachers of the diamond laid out at the south end of the village green, sipping Budweisers. High above the green, a snipe winnowed its way down the twilit sky, its wings whis-tling. Charlie mimicked a hunter raising a shotgun. "Bang!"

"No more blind dates," Jim said.

"She teaches girls' phys ed over at Theenie's school," Charlie said. "A real outdoorswoman, Jimbo, very healthful lifestyle, the build of a Norse goddess. She may be Norwegian, for all I know. Her first name's Hildy. She saw you play ball a few years ago over at the university. She wants to take you on a hike up Jay Peak. She belongs to the Green Mountain Club, the Appalachian Club, has two hundred and twelve species on her bird life-list—"

"I don't keep life-lists and I hate to hike for the sake of hik-ing," Jim said. "I have to have a destination, like a trout pond."

"Hildy's an expert fly-fisher. Also, she loves to travel. She's traveled to Alaska and British Columbia."

"Good for her. Tell Hildy I've traveled much in Kingdom County."

"Very funny, Henry David. I think she's had her eye on you for a while. She could support you with her teacher's salary and you could quit your day job at the paper and write your own stories fulltime."

"I don't want to quit my job at the paper. That's where my material comes from."

For a time the brothers sipped their beer and said nothing. In the Kingdom it was not unusual for your best friend also to be a sibling. Jim and Charlie were comfortable together talking or not talking. They always had been.

"Why is it," Jim said, "that married people want everybody else to be married?"

"I don't know," Charlie said. "It speaks well for the married state. Can you imagine where I'd be if Theenie hadn't taken me in hand? Probably in jail. Or dead."

"I don't want to be taken in hand," Jim said. "Not by a Norse goddess named Hildy. Not by anybody. Hey, it seemed good to take a swipe at a baseball again. Down in Boston I didn't have time to play. Tell Hildy, meaning no disrespect, that I'm not ready to date yet. Maybe Betsy was right. Maybe I never will be."

Sunday at noon, when they reached the top of Jay Peak, Jim felt as though he'd been walked into the ground. Hildy was as sturdy as a pulling pony at Kingdom Fair. She glowed with good health and purposefulness. They'd fished up the mountain on the Jay Branch, where she'd caught four trout to his one. On their way she'd added a rare carnivorous sundew to her life-list of boreal alpine plants. At first Jim thought she might be having a religious epiphany over the discovery. The day before Hildy had attended the Outlaws home opener

against the Landing. "Just one small tip," Hildy told him after
the game. "When you bat? Keep your hands back a split second longer. You'll find you drive the ball harder."

Jim had gone three for four with two long line-drive dou-
bles. He had looked at Charlie, who shrugged and grinned.

Now, high on the mountain, looking out over the forests of
four different states and a huge swath of Quebec, they made a
small fire and ate fried trout with bread and butter and strong
tea. Hildy said grace. Afterward she inquired if he had been
saved.

Jim said that most of the Kinnesons, including himself, were
freethinking apostates and beyond help in that department.
Hildy said no one was beyond Jesus' help if they would come
to him with a humble heart. Her eyes glowed with evangelical
fervor and something more besides.

Lately Jim had imagined that he heard Frannie's voice in his
head. "Quick," his former girlfriend said, "tell her the last time
you called on Jesus for help he was off dynamiting trout with
the Chosen Twelve."

"Will you please be quiet?" Jim said.

"What?" Hildy said. "Listen, there are different ways to be
saved. I can put you in the mood right now."

"Run for the hills," Frannie's voice said in his head. "The
woman means to have her way with you. Go, before she places
you in some kind of submission hold and it's too late."

The gym teacher began to unbutton her L.L. Bean hiking
shirt. She did not seem to be wearing a bra. Could Charlie be
in on all this? Or even Athena? No. In her athletic way Hildy
was very attractive. Why not? It would take his mind off his
phantom former girlfriend.

"We'll have our own little decathlon," Hildy said, giggling.

Nearby, someone gave out a long yodel, like a rooster crowing. "Hello, folks," a voice said. "Nice day for a hike."

A young man and woman dressed up like Swiss mountaineers stood on the trail a few feet away. They wore leather knee pants, Birkenstocks, bright red vests over green shirts, caps with feathers.

"Are we interrupting something?" the young woman said.

Jim jumped to his feet. "Not at all," he said.

Hildy was buttoning up her shirt.

On their way back down the mountain, Jim and Hildy couldn't help bursting out laughing—laughing at themselves mainly. Jim liked this girl very much, as he had Betsy. There was only one difficulty.

She wasn't Frannie.

Sometimes Jim took a weekend and canoed up to the Kinneson family hunting and fishing cabin on the Upper Kingdom River. There in the ancestral camp, where he'd gone with his father and Charlie and his grandfather, James Kinneson II, he fished the river for his beloved brook trout, explored the surrounding wilderness, and worked on his collection of stories. He'd begun sending out individual pieces to small magazines, mostly literary reviews and quarterlies. One evening in May he returned from camp to find a package containing six copies of a respected Midwestern review containing a story he'd submitted months ago and nearly given up hope for. It was called "A Diminished Thing," a line from Frost's celebrated poem "The Ovenbird." In it, against the background of a Vermont village like Kingdom

Common that had lost its furniture factory, its Academy, and most of its surrounding farms, with a hand-lettered sign at the village limits, buried under snow half of the year, that said, PLEASE, OUR TOWN NEEDS A DOCTOR, he told the story of his yearlong romance with Frannie. No one from the review had even contacted him to tell him they'd accepted his submission. There it was, his first published fiction. He could scarcely have been happier had he won the Nobel Prize.

To celebrate Jim's news, his brother and sister-in-law took him to dinner at the hotel. Over Armand St. Onge's locally famous *porc sucre d'erable* and poutine, and Molson's that Armand still smuggled into the Kingdom from Canada, with its higher octane and yeastier flavor, Charlie produced a copy of the *Memphremagog Express* from his briefcase. "Ladies and gentlemen of the jury," he said, may I direct your attention to Exhibit A." He opened the paper, and read aloud:

Dear Lonely Hearts,
   Young man, midtwenties, in literary profession, loves fishing, walking in the rain, long fireside chats. Looking for companionship, commitment. Sense of humor a must.
                                            Seventh-generation Vermonter

"What's this about?" Jim said. "You want to hook me up with a man? What do you know about me that I don't know about myself?"

"You're missing the point," Charlie said. He handed the newspaper to Jim. "Read it for yourself."

Jim scanned the letter. "Christ Jesus, Charlie. This is me, isn't it?"

"Charlie, you are insane," Athena said. "I should have gone the lonely-hearts route myself."

"Not at all," Charlie said. "I gave my own P. O. box. No one will ever guess who it is."

"This takes the cake," Jim said. "I'll never mention dating again. I'll go into the woods and build a pillar like Simeon Stylites. I'll live the life of an anchorite." He was laughing despite himself.

"Don't try to change the subject, bub," Charlie said. "I'll screen the applicants. Just pass along the cream of the crop to you."

Jim said, "What do you hear from Frannie, Miss Athena? Still engaged to be engaged?"

"She's finishing up her residency in psychiatry," Athena said. "Out in Vancouver. I think she's engaged to be engaged to someone new. She's as picky as you are, Jimmy."

"Let's not start up with Frannie again," Charlie said. "I could never figure out what you saw in her in the first place, Jim. You never knew what she'd say next. I married an outspoken woman and look what I've been reduced to. This weekend, Jimmy. Ste. Catherine Street. I'll chaperone—"

"You aren't going within a country mile of Ste. Catherine Street, buster," Athena said. "Not this weekend, not any weekend. As your wonderful dad would say, that's the beginning and the end of it."

Over the next couple of weeks Charlie passed along to Jim a letter from a young woman veterinarian in Pond in the Sky who specialized in rescuing and rehabilitating stray and mistreated animals. She owned eleven dogs, nineteen cats, and a six-foot-long reticulated python. "Must love critters," she stipulated, which Jim did, though not quite enough to respond. Another correspondent wrote declaring that she too was a writer. Did he have an agent and if so would he be willing to share their name? (No and no.)

"Listen to this, Jim," Charlie said. " 'Just out of school. Shy but passionate. Discover for yourself.' "

"She's probably all of thirteen," Jim said. "This may seem strange, but I'd rather not spend the next ten years writing stories from a jail cell."

"I'll find out who she is and run a background check," Charlie said.

"Who's meeting this crazed waif, you or your brother?" Athena said. "You're becoming altogether too personally invested in these idiotic assignations, Charlie."

Just then Doc Harrison, Prof. Chadburn, and Jim and Charlie's dad, Editor Kinneson came in, stomping the spring snow off their feet. They sat down at an adjacent table and ordered a round of Armand's contraband Molsons to toast Jim and his maiden publication.

"Your 'Our town needs a doctor' sign's going to be buried out of sight if this keeps up, Doc," Charlie said. "Any luck yet?"

"I've been advertising in the medical journals, too," Doc said. "But no. I can't seem to find anyone who wants to starve to death up here at the far end of nowhere. Even for a full partnership with the option to buy me out for a song. How you doing, Miss Athena?"

"All systems seem to be on go," Athena said, patting her midriff. "Seven months left and counting."

Jim looked at Charlie. For once in his life, his older brother seemed thunderstruck. "I'll be damned," he said.

"That, too, no doubt," principal Athena said. Then, "You're going to be an uncle, Jimmy. If it's a boy, we'll name him for you."

When Jim finally wrote back to "Shy But Passionate" in what he regarded as something akin to an act of desperation, though he could not seem to prevent himself from doing so, she agreed to meet him in the hotel dining room for drinks and dinner on a Friday evening in early June. It was lilac time in Kingdom Common, and at last the snow was gone. The High Falls was just a faint echo of its former self during runoff, and the peeper frogs were singing along the marshy banks of the Lower Kingdom River like the jingle of so many sleigh bells. In streams all over the Kingdom brook trout were biting like mad.

As Friday night approached Jim felt alternately apprehensive and strangely hopeful. Somehow he felt that she must be gorgeous, like Frannie and her cousin Athena. By the weekend he was dying to "discover for himself."

Jim was waiting at the hotel at 6:30. He'd brought a cut-glass vase of yellow roses cut from his mother's old-fashioned Harrisons. Later a country band would set up on the small stage at one end of the bar and couples would two-step and waltz to songs immortalized by Hank Williams, Patsy Cline, and Lefty Frizzell. Armand's Molsons would be in high demand and as much French as English would be spoken in the dining room of the hotel. This was the world Jim wrote about, the world he loved. But what would "Shy But Passionate" think? Two years ago he had invited a young woman, a pretty graduate teaching assistant at Harvard, to spend a weekend at his parents' farmhouse across the river. He'd brought her to a dance at the hotel, and she'd fled back to Cambridge on the first morning train.

Seven o'clock came and went with no sign of Jim's pen pal. At a little after eight Charlie and Athena stopped by and sat down at Jim's table to commiserate with him. Athena looked at the yellow roses, then at Jim. Only when he saw his own expression reflected on her face did he realize how disappointed he was. He grinned at his brother and sister-in-law and shrugged.

"To hell with her then," Charlie said. "It's her loss. Tell you what, bud. How's about you and I spend the weekend up at camp? I can't come in until tomorrow afternoon but you can paddle up in the Old Town in the morning and I'll row up in the bateau as soon as I can get off. We'll catch some brookies, drink some beer, clear our heads of all this. No more lonelyhearts letters, I promise. You'll find who you're looking for when the right time comes."

Jim wasn't so sure. Nor did he feel much like going up to the hunting and fishing camp, which was where he and Frannie had first made love. But he couldn't possibly avoid every place where they'd done that. In their short year together they'd made love all over the Kingdom.

"How's young Jim?" Jim said to Athena.

Athena smiled. "Young Jim turned out to be young Ruthie—after your wonderful mom. She's fine."

"Now that I'm going to be a father," Charlie said. "I realize better than ever that life goes on and has to go on. Not going fishing with your brother may protect you from the humiliation of being outfished three trout to one the way you were by the Norsewoman. It won't help you get over that scheming French tart that ditched you a decade ago. You have to stop basking in your broken heart, son. See you at camp. Around midafternoon. Any small yellow mayfly ought to be deadly this time of year. We'll hit the evening hatch, clean up."

The following dawn Jim slid Gramp's green canvas Old Town into the bed of his pickup and drove up the River Road to Pond Number One in the Chain of Ponds just south of the border. Trout were rising to the surface but Jim had much larger quarry in mind, the big red Canadian squaretails that lived in the icy depths of Three and the mile of alternating whitewater and swirling green pools between Three and the big lake. This time of year a streamer fly known as a Little Brook Trout because that is what it resembled was irresistible to the cannibalistic lunkers in the river.

By the time he was paddling up the west shoreline of Three, Jim was glad he'd come. He could never remember a time when he hadn't experienced some elevated sense of well-being from going to the woods or out onto the remote ponds and rivers of the Kingdom. He angled the bow of the canoe toward a headland beyond which the camp, still invisible, sat one hundred yards up the slope from the shore in a mixed stand of hardwoods whose fresh new leaves were still more yellow than green. As he rounded the headland, he caught, on the morning breeze, the unmistakable tang of woodsmoke. He hadn't checked to see if the old lumbering bateau was upside down under a tarp in the same spruce trees where he'd launched the Old Town on One. Maybe Charlie'd gotten away early after all.

But the bateau wasn't visible near the small landing dock in front of the camp. It wasn't unusual for other fishermen or hunters, known or unknown, to use the Kinneson camp for a night or two. The door was left unlocked year-round. Leave the woodbox full for the next party was the code. That was all. Jim wondered where the fire-builder might be. Probably off fishing some remote cove of the pond out of sight from the camp.

He ran the canoe onto the gravel strip beside the spruce-pole dock and headed up toward the porch. He always remembered the camp as bigger than it was because it had seemed large to him as a boy. "Charlie?" he called out. "That you?"

Frannie Lafleur stepped out onto the porch. She was wearing a red hunting jacket, denim slacks, rubber-bottomed hunting pacs laced halfway to the top of their leather uppers, a red-and-black checked flannel shirt beneath the jacket. Her raven hair hung straight to her waist and her lavender eyes, the color of wildwood violets, were full of humor.

"Hello, James," she said. "You look surprised. Who did you expect? One of your little lonely-heart harlots no doubt. 'Shy But Passionate,' or one of her sorry ilk. Oh, yes. Cousin Athena has kept me all too well informed concerning your latest capers. Will you shake hands with me? Or do you intend to stand there and pout for a year or two?"

They shook hands as they had long ago on the granite steps of the Academy on the day they first met. Frannie continued to hold his hand in hers as she said, in her musical French accent, "*Eh, bien*. I can plainly see why no physician would wish to settle up here. Just as I remember, it's the end of the known world. You must know, James, that I spoke with our good Dr. Harrison last evening. We made, he and I, a bargain. He needs a partner, someone to take over when he retires. I need a practice to start out in. Do you still carouse every evening at that so-called hotel with your insane brother, swilling Molsons? That will soon come to a screeching halt, a bit of preventive medicine."

Jim well remembered from their high school days that Frannie liked to drink a cold one in the evening herself. Not so much, though, as she liked to tease him. She still held his hand firmly in hers.

"Do you remember those wicked schoolgirls who called me a nigger on my first day at the Academy? I will become their personal physician and kill them with kindness."

"I thought you were studying to be a psychiatrist," Jim said, returning the pressure on his hand.

"I am a psychiatrist. Surely you know that a psychiatrist is an M.D. before she is a psychiatrist. It so happens that the hospital in Memphremagog needs a consulting psychiatrist two afternoons a week. Of course they will hire me. Do you have any idea what a field day I'll have up here in the Kingdom, James? It's a treasure chest of serious mental and emotional disorders."

"And stories."

"Yes, disorders and stories."

Out on Three a loon hooted. Frannie hooted back, her call indistinguishable from the loon's. Jim's heart turned over in his chest.

"Are you still engaged to be engaged?" Jim blurted out.

"Hardly," Frannie said as though such a notion was absurd. "*Écoute-vous*, James. I've kept close track of you and your antics. Cousin Athena sent me that story you wrote. About the silly young French girl and the boy who for unknown reasons loved her."

Frannie gave his hand a tug, like a trout. "Come inside," she said. "I suppose you will remember the first time we came here?"

"I do."

It was as though they'd never been apart. They came together in each other's arms and five minutes later they were making love in the sleeping loft, as they had on that long-ago day when they were seventeen.

Afterward, Jim told her, to her great delight, about his lonely-hearts dates.

" 'Shy But Passionate,' was me," Frannie said. "Don't you think I'm shy, James?"

"What about all those guys you were engaged to be engaged to?"

"None of them ever wrote a love story about me. Also, I think you may have just made me pregnant. Now we'll have to get married and spend the rest of our lives together in this wasteland."

Jim kissed her and they made love again, slower but just as passionately. "My," Frannie said when they finished this time, "I can see you are still the incorrigible romantic, James. That's what I've always loved most about you. You haven't changed at all."

"Everything changes. It's the first law of nature. You told me so the day we went our separate ways."

Frannie thought. Then she smiled and said, "For once in my life—just once—I was wrong. Love never changes. I realized that when I read your story. Come, Mr. Lonely Hearts. I'll prove it to you."

8

Dispossessed

For sixty years and more, on Memorial Day weekend, Jim Kinneson and his brother Charlie had made the canoe run together. They put in by the Canadian border, in the Great Northern Bog where the river rose, and paddled down through the bog and the gore to the family hunting and fishing camp on Pond Number Three. After spending the night at the camp, they canoed and fished their way to the mouth of the river where it emptied into the big lake, Memphremagog. It was a thirteen-mile paddle past seven mountains, so they had always called their two-day canoe trek the Seven Mountain Run. Sometimes Charlie jokingly referred to their annual expedition as a "two-rig fish" because they would leave Charlie's pickup at the trailhead on Monadnock Mountain and carry the Old Town the three miles through the woods to the bog and fish their way down to Jim's pickup at the mouth of the river. They could have accomplished the trip in one long day. But they preferred to take their time, fishing as they went, and they loved staying over at camp, which went back in the family seven generations to Charles Kinneson I, their great-great-great-great-grandfather.

They left Jim's beater in a pull-off beside the river's mouth the evening before and headed east out the county road before dawn the next morning with Gramp's green Old Town in the bed of Charlie's rig, turned north in Pond in the Sky, and arrived at the trailhead at sunrise. It was misting a little so they put on their rain jackets and rain pants to hike in through the wet bush to the bog. The light rain wouldn't hurt the fishing at all. The trout should be feeding hard in the morning rain. Jim's Nikon, which he used mainly to take pictures for the *Monitor*, was wrapped in an oilcloth inside his waterproof knapsack. The Nikon was safe from the rain. The rain pants were a little cumbersome but no one wanted to sit in a canoe all day with a wet behind. If the sun popped out later, they could take off their raingear and fold it up and stick it under the bow with the knapsack containing the camera.

Almost no one other than a few stalwart deer hunters in the fall of the year used the game trail over the shoulder of Monadnock. It dead-ended at the edge of the bog, a few hundred feet south of the border. As for the bog and the gore and the river, the brothers had a much better chance of sighting a pine marten or a Canada lynx there than another human being. The Great Northern Bog, which stretched across the border deep into the Quebec forest, was the haunt of three-toed and black-backed woodpeckers, spruce grouse, lemmings, and Canada jays, none of which were found elsewhere in Vermont. In the winter it was visited by gyrfalcons and great gray owls with yellow eyes as deep and unknowable as the boreal heart of the bog.

At eighty, ten years older than Jim, Charlie was a far cry from the tireless, sure-footed boy who'd run up and down these mountains at twenty but he insisted on carrying the Old Town alone, upside down on his shoulders, as always. For his age, or any age, he was still rugged. He stood mid-thwart with his legs slightly bent beside the canoe and with a hand on each gunnel lifted it to rest on his upper thighs, then jerked it over his head and turned it upside down in one smooth motion, tilting up at a shallow angle with the gunnels now resting on his shoulders and his hands on the gunnels just in front of his head. It was an impressive demonstration. Jim, excellent in the woods himself and a decade younger, wasn't sure he could still do it. Jim came along behind Charlie with the three packs, one in each hand, one on his back. The trail was steep, worn down by moose and deer traffic to the bare reddish roots of spruce and cedar trees. In places hobblebush, with its large purplish leaves and treacherous roots good for nothing but tripping over and snapping an ankle like kindle-wood, had encroached on the trail. Delicate white Canada mayflowers with raspberry-colored throats were still in blossom here on the back side of the mountain. On the north sides of boulders pockets of snow lay covered with brown hemlock needles.

Charlie stumbled twice. "Look out, Clarence Darrow," Jim said. "If you break your neck I'll never get you out of here."

"Sure you will," Charlie said.

Despite himself, Jim bit. "How?"

"Same way the old Frenchman did the bull moose he shot," Charlie said in his most exaggerated Canuck accent. "Make t'ree, four trip."

Charlie roared over his joke, filling the surrounding woods

with his laughter. From somewhere on the ridgeline, a pileated woodpecker hammered on a tree like a mad axeman, as if in response. To this day Jim loved going to the woods with his brother the judge. There was only one Charlie. The question was, which one? The longtime district judge, the shrewdest adjudicator in Vermont, whose motto—his crude Frenchmen jokes notwithstanding—could have come directly off the Statue of Liberty? Or the Kingdom County home boy who fished and hunted when he wanted to, in season and out, and drank beer for breakfast at camp?

Charlie stopped beside an icy rill, a step-across-in-one-step brook, spilling down the mountainside next to the game trail. Reversing the lifting process, he set the canoe down and knelt to drink out of the brook from his cupped hands. Jim too drank from his hands. He loved thinking that he still lived in a place where the running water in a brook was safe to drink although you had to be sure that there wasn't a beaver dam upstream. You didn't want to contract the virulent local dysentery known as beaver fever. He was pretty sure the rill was pure. It was too small for beaver works. Yellow and black Canadian swallowtails drifted down the narrow open corridor in the trees above the game trail. Several of the butterflies landed beside a muddy declivity in the trail next to a bower of rare pink lady's-slippers. The swallowtails were opening and closing their wings, still damp and glistening from the cocoon, and sipping up minerals from the mud. Jim got out the Nikon and took a close-up of the swallowtails drinking. He showed Charlie the image in the viewfinder and Charlie nodded.

"You know what I'd have done to those butterflies when I was about eight?" Charlie said.

"No, and I don't want to," Jim said.

"Boys," Charlie said.

Jim knew all about boys. He and Frannie'd raised two of them. Charlie and Athena'd had one daughter, no sons, but Charlie'd been a second father to Armand and Lucien, set them and their Cousin Freeman Kinneson up in their outfitting business in Montana. Ruthie, Charlie and Athena's daughter, was an ACLU attorney in Washington.

"Excuse me, folks. This land is posted. Sorry. It's for liability reasons."

The two strangers, middle-aged, were putting up posted signs on the northeast side of the brook. They wore green plastic rain ponchos with Army Corps of Engineers decals on the shoulders. The signs read NO HUNTING, FISHING, TRAPPING, HIKING OR TRESPASSING. VIOLATORS WILL BE PROSECUTED TO THE FULLEST EXTENT OF THE LAW. U. S. ARMY ENGINEERS.

Charlie set down the canoe. "Good morning, gentlemen. What Vermont law actually says, begging your pardon, is that 'no flowing waters within the boundaries of the State of Vermont can be posted or otherwise closed off or barred to the public.' Now, the last I checked, yup, this brook is flowing. So we'll just splash on down it and put in the canoe where it runs into the bog and never set foot on your property at all. Long as we're in the brook, you won't have any liability to worry about."

"Look, we aren't trying to pick a fight," the other man said. "But you're standing on federal land right now. If you'll just walk back up out again, we certainly wouldn't press charges. Otherwise, we'll have to leave it up to the local judge."

Charlie picked up the canoe again and stepped into the brook. Jim was pretty sure he knew what was coming next.

"Why don't you come down and stop us?" Charlie said. "No need to bother the judge. I'm sure he has more important matters to deal with. We'll settle up right here."

In his younger days Charlie was always inviting someone or other to step outside and "settle up." So far as Jim knew, his brother hadn't been constrained to settle up with anyone in the grand old Kingdom County tradition for a number of years. Jim wanted to unlimber his fly rod and get out on the water. This had gone far enough.

"I'm Jim Kinneson, editor of the local newspaper," he said. "This is my brother, Charlie Kinneson, who happens to be the local judge. If you have a complaint, contact the state's attorney. But Charlie's right about the brook. You can't post running water."

One of the strangers shook his head and said to his partner, "I told you we shouldn't come up here without a deputy sheriff." He mumbled something about the movie. Deliverance. Charlie laughed. "Tell the judge," he called back. "Me and this other man here have an appointment with some native eastern brook trout."

Jim laughed. The "me and this other man here" was a long-standing private joke between the brothers. When Jim was ten or eleven, Charlie, home on break from law school, loved to take him over to the barroom of the Common Hotel for a soda pop. They'd sit at a table overlooking the village green and Charlie'd rap his knuckles on the table and call out to Armand St. Onge, "Monsieur Barkeep. Bring me and this other man here two cold ones if you please." A minute later, Armand would appear with a bottle of beer for Charlie and a Nehi or Coke for Jim. Jim had loved being called a man by his big brother, who treated him more like a fishing partner or best friend than a kid. For as long as he could remember, that's what he and Charlie had been. Best friends and fishing partners.

"I thought I was gong to have a Friar Tuck–Little John situation on my hands back there," Jim said.

"Cut me a quarterstaff," Charlie roared. "Ironwood, preferably."

Twenty minutes later the brook was deepening and the banks were becoming aldery. They were nearing the bog.

"Can they legally keep us from fishing?" Jim said.

"They can try," Charlie said. "I wouldn't want to prevent me from fishing the place my great-great-great-great-grandfather discovered two hundred and fifty years ago."

"Times have changed since then."

"You can say that again," Charlie said.

"I suppose they'd say they were just doing their job," Jim said.

"So are we," Charlie said. "Our job as Kinnesons is to keep them from keeping us from doing our jobs."

Jim laughed. On a knoll ahead sat a partly collapsed log building overlooking the bog and the mountains encircling it. The bog had been created about ten thousand years ago by the glacier, which had sheared off the mountains overlooking it and carved out a great watery bowl of boreal sedges and wildflowers, beaver runs, flows, marshy verges, and mixed stands of hardwood and soft interspersed by kettle ponds and backwaters leading nowhere. The bog was a beautiful and treacherous place.

Nailed to the lintel log over the missing door of the partially caved-in cabin was a board into which long ago someone had carved the words CAMP NO. 7. In the early days of lumbering in the bog and the gore both the logging camps and the mountains were commonly referred to by numbers. Monadnock Mountain was Number 7, so too the logging camp at its base.

"Picture?" Charlie said.

Jim set down the packs and got out his Nikon. The mizzling rain had moved along to the east and sunshine was trying to break through, hazy in the mist rising from the bog. The light was perfect. Jim could get the camp in the foreground with the smoking bog and two more peaks, Six and Five, in the background.

Of course, there was a story about Camp Number Seven. Gramp had told it to Charlie and Jim when as young boys they first began coming to the Great Northern Bog to fish and hunt, to blueberry on the slopes above its fringes in August and cranberry along its waterways in October. According to Gramp, the fabled walking boss on the annual Upper Kingdom log drive, Noël Lord, had in his employ a riverboy who habitually overslept the cookie's 4:30 A.M. wakeup triangle. Finally Noël'd had a bellyful of the tardy jack. He stepped into the camp, shook the sleeper awake, jerked him upright in his bunk, then tossed a quarter stick of dynamite onto the red-hot lid of the camp stove. Noël emerged from the camp with the riverboy flying out the door behind him seconds before the entire stove blew out the back wall of the camp. Jim had tried to pry the quarter stick of dynamite anecdote into more than one of his stories but maddeningly had never found a way to make it fit. Anecdotes that didn't fit into a story organically stood out as conspicuously as a black eye. He made a mental note to somehow use the tale in his current book-in-progress. At seventy, if he wanted to shoehorn in a logging anecdote, he by God would.

"Hey, bubba. You writing in your head again?"

Jim had taken the picture half a minute ago. He grinned.

"Let's get this show on the road," Charlie said. "We've got miles to go before we sleep, *Frère Jacques*. Hop in the bow. Otherwise—boom boom. *Le* T.N.T."

As usual when they made their annual Seven Mountain Run, the brothers began by paddling north a few hundred yards in the narrow winding channel through the bog to the border. The international border was designated by a thirty-foot-wide cleared strip through the forest, with Canadian granite obelisks set every several hundred yards. Here on one of the wildest and most remote stretches of the boundary between Canada and the United States the once-cleared strip had grown back up and blended into the surrounding woods. The granite obelisks as well were long gone. French Canadian and Yankee farmers along the Line had found them useful for porch steps, cellar foundations, stone walls. There had been no border when Jim and Charlie's Abenaki great-great-great-great-grandmother, Charles I's wife Molly Molasses, came here in her birch canoe to fish and hunt and berry. The border was just an idea, a bad one in the opinion of the Clan Kinneson and their neighbors in Vermont and Quebec. They'd always shopped across it, gone to church and school across it, married across it like Jim and Frannie. Mainly, they'd ignored it.

The Old Town glided through the narrow channel of running water in the bog. Twice they had to put out and drag it over beaver dams. The extensive beaver works and downed tamaracks and cedars prevented most canoeists from exploring the bog. It was too much trouble to get past them. Jim and Charlie expected to get their feet wet.

Here in the far reaches of the Great Northern Bog the brothers' Memphremagog ancestors had tried to retreat from Charles Kinneson and Rogers Rangers. A few escaped, including Molly, who would later marry Charles I. Most were hunted down and slaughtered. Here, too, Charles's son James I and a handful of secessionists, pursued by federal troops in 1812, simply vanished into the unbroken northern swampland and forest. "Rebel Jim" and fewer than one hundred Kingdom loggers, river drivers, hardscrabble farmers, trappers, and smugglers had maintained the independence of the Kingdom Republic from Vermont and the Union for the next thirty years over the issue of slavery, which they had outlawed in the Kingdom from the start. When the insurrectionists lured the federal militia deep into the morass and ambushed them, wearing kilts and screeching "Remember Culloden," the Continental Army "went back to Boston faster than they'd come up," according to the account of the battle in Pliny Templeton's great *Ecclesiastical, Natural, Social, and Political History of Kingdom County.* In 1864, after stealing $100,000 from the Bank of Kingdom Common in the northernmost action of the Civil War, Captain Bennett Young, CSA, and his twenty Confederate raiders had retreated back into Canada on the old Canada Post Road along the edge of the bog. During Prohibition, Charlie and Jim's grandfather, James Kinneson II, had run

Canadian booze down the Post Road. The bog was nothing if not a repository of Kingdom and Kinneson history. Fugitive slaves by the hundreds passed through it, with the help of Rebel Jim and his son, Charles II. Some stopped there, establishing the granite quarry at the foot of Canada Mountain until they were burned out by the Vermont Ku Klux Klan.

It was still early in the morning but the emerging sun was burning the mist off the surface of the water. Jim sat in the bow. Charlie, thirty pounds heavier and built like an NFL wide receiver, paddled from the stern. Around a bend a moose stood up to its belly, watching them motionlessly from the sedges beside the channel. Jim pointed with his paddle. *"L'original,"* Charlie said, which is what the early French explorers who came to North America had named these ungainly-looking but perfectly adapted North Woods members of the deer family.

"L'original, all right," Jim said, laughing. Charlie pointed an imaginary gun at the moose. "Bang." Charles was still an avid hunter. Jim would no more shoot a moose or a deer than a beloved farm horse. Yet it was Jim who'd inherited Gramp's nearly preternatural woods skills.

It was time to begin fishing. The brothers removed from their cylindrical aluminum cases the Orvis Battenkills Gramp had given each of them, in turn, when they'd graduated from college. They attached their two-ounce Hardy reels and cream-colored floating line and tied on size-twelve Royal Coachman flies, red and white creations resembling no natural insect but rather the fry of the trout themselves. Brook trout were savagely cannibalistic.

"Go ahead," Jim said.

"Where?"

Jim studied the channel, reading the water like a scholar deciphering a palimpsest from some old, old ruins. "Ten feet above the muskrat house. By that larch stob. An underwater spring comes in there."

Charlie made a couple of false casts, dropped his Coachman a foot from the jutting stick. It sank an inch below the surface. He gave it a twitch. "Fish on," he called out. Jim reached behind his canoe seat for the landing net. A minute later he netted a ten-inch brookie which he unhooked and released. It was too early in the day to begin keeping fish for supper.

Once again, as the brothers canoed the bog, Jim felt the sense of ineffable pleasure he experienced in the woods or on good water with his brother and fishing partner. Jim's wife, Dr. Frannie Lafleur Kinneson, had told him that she felt that same contented connectedness at the ocean. At one time, after the glaciers that carved out the bog had melted and withdrawn, the Great Northern Bog was connected to the ocean by vast arms of fresh water stretching deep into what would become Vermont from the St. Lawrence River.

For the rest of the morning they paddled by easy stages south through the bog, past the bases of Sixth, Fifth, Fourth mountains. They passed two more former logging bunkhouses now used as deer and fishing camps but saw no signs of the owners.

At noon, where the Black Branch stole noiselessly into the Upper West Branch, they ate smoked ham and five-year-old Cabot cheese sandwiches they'd put up the night before, washed down by tall boys in red, white, and blue cans. For dessert, wedges of Frannie's strawberry pie, then strong black tea boiled in an empty coffee can beside the junction of the two streams. The wind had shifted around to the northwest, portending clear weather. There was just enough stir in the air to keep off the black flies and mosquitoes.

The brothers had a second cup of tea. While they ate they said little. They were comfortable talking or not. Also there was an unspoken agreement between them, a list of topics they rarely discussed on their outings. Matters having to do with health and aging. Financial considerations. The electronic era. More recently, the future of the Great Northern Bog and the gore. The future in general. The past was fair game. At least in the Kingdom, and in the stories Jim wrote, the past was still very much a part of the present.

"Let's pay the cranes a visit," Charlie said when they'd finished their tea. "Bring your camera."

Jim leading the way with his Nikon, they walked up a faint game trail beside the Black Branch. Here the tributary was little more than a seep through the alders and willows. Farther inland there was a little lift to the terrain and the brook purled down over dark mossy stones. A few trout fry darted away like miniature torpedoes. They came out of the alders beside an ancient dead beaver pond stretching several hundred yards to some cliffs at the base of Fifth Mountain. Here in a starkly beautiful otherworldly region the Great Blue Herons known locally as blue cranes had built their messy stick nests in the tops of long-dead tamarack trees jutting high over the inky water. The young herons, two or three to a nest, were clamoring to be fed by adult birds hunting fish, frogs, and voles along the marge of the old beaver flow. It was a strange and wondrous scene, perhaps forty birds in all, unchanged from a prehistoric era predating even the Abenakis and the glaciers. As Jim photographed the herons, showing Charlie each image in the viewfinder, it occurred to him that the cranes probably hadn't changed themselves much in millions of years. With their long slender yellow legs that dangled behind them in flight like vestigial tails, they seemed somehow an emblem of permanence. Jim knew that he was projecting his own romantic outlook onto the universe. Still, he couldn't help smiling, in admiration, at the clever joke of evolution that had resulted in herons. His smile widened. At seventy, he'd think them good-humored even if he didn't know better. Their long yellow bill was as sharp as a barber's razor and, if cornered, they'd drive it clean through a man's hand. That's how genial they were. Jim loved the herons.

On a bare-limbed dead cedar at the upper end of the dead bog sat an osprey, its head white as a bald eagle's in the June sunshine. An eagle might have taken a young heron, but not so the fish-eating osprey. How the herons understood that the osprey was of no danger to them, no one knew. They simply did. Some old-time Kingdom woodsmen considered ospreys to be hard on the trout population though most would not dream of shooting one.

The brothers returned to the canoe and paddled on into the blue afternoon. Where Little Quebec Brook spilled into the West Branch they caught and kept two foot-long trout apiece for supper. They traversed the north end of Pond Number Three and ran the Old Town up onto the gravel and sand apron just below the family camp, which Jim photographed from the shore of the pond. Kingdom Mountain rose steep in the background and, across the outlet of the pond, its twin, Canada Mountain.

The brothers cleaned their trout on the gravel beside the pond. As always, they checked the contents of their stomachs to see what the fish had been feeding on: mayflies, hellgrammites, one bright emerald inchworm, a few tiny trout. Brook trout didn't have scales so you didn't need to scrape them. As Gramp had loved to remind Jim and Charlie, brook trout weren't "true" trout but rather landlocked Arctic char. They too had come down from the Far North with the glacier, found the boreal Kingdom suitable to their needs, and stayed on. Like the Kinnesons themselves, Gramp had told Jim and Charlie.

They strung the gutted fish on a forked tag alder stick and carried them and their knapsacks up the slope to the camp overlooking the pond. Charlie, leading the way, stopped short. "Whoa!" he shouted, as though he'd been about to step on a rattlesnake. Charlie gestured up at the camp with the trout on the alder branch. At first Jim didn't know what he was pointing at. Then, stapled to the door, he saw the notice, printed on the same heavy yellow paper as the posted signs the two officials they'd encountered earlier were tacking up. THESE PREMISES HAVE BEEN CONDEMNED BY THE ARMY CORPS OF ENGINEERS, it read, then went on to reiterate that trespassers would be prosecuted to the full extent of the law.

The brothers walked up onto the porch. A large shiny padlock hung from the rusted hasp on the door. "Picture," Charlie said. Jim was already rummaging in the pack for the Nikon.

While Jim got the shot, Charlie fetched the splitting axe

from the woodshed. He knocked the hasp and the new lock off the camp door with one short blow with the back of the axe-head. Wordlessly, he tore down the "condemned" poster. In-side the camp he crumpled the poster into a ball and threw it into the cold firebox of the Glenwood.

"Kindle," he said.

Jim looked at his brother. He glanced around the camp, built two hundred years ago by their great-great-great-grandfather, his namesake James "Rebel Jim" Kinneson I. He said some-thing, not quite audible.

"Say what?" Charlie said.

"Dispossessed," Jim said a little louder. "We've been dis-possessed."

They returned to the family camp once more in the fall to clean it out. It was opening week of deer season but Jim had given up hunting decades ago and Charlie had no interest in going alone. Construction on the dam would begin in the spring. Next year by the opening of deer season the Great Northern Bog and the gore and the camp would all be under one hundred feet of water. They didn't stay overnight.

Four months ago Charlie'd stood in the well of the United States Supreme Court giving his PowerPoint presentation. Jim sat in the gallery with his reporter's pad. Though he'd taken the slides, seen them twenty times, he was still spell-bound. Charlie'd selected only a handful, and decided against an accompanying narrative. One or two words identifying each image would be more effective.

"Lady's-slippers. Eastern brook trout. Bog Rosemary. Black ducks. Old Town canoe. Heronry."

"Hold that slide for a moment, please, Mr. Kinneson. The herons. Where will they go?"

"I don't know, Justice Thompson. I don't know where they'll go. Away."

"So they'll find another nesting place?"

"I suppose so. Not like this one. There's only one Great Northern Bog. You know"—he was having a conversation with the justices now, the way he'd conversed with juries for half a century and more—"you know, the Engineer Corps wants flood control. Fine. Nobody likes floods. But the Great Northern Bog provides the best flood control imaginable. It's a gigantic natural sponge. It sops up all the rainwater and snowmelt, then releases it gradually over the course of the year."

"Mr. Kinneson, in the end, aren't the 'Friends of the Great Northern Bog' just trying to save the bog for nobody and no reason?"

"Not at all, Justice White. I'd sooner say the Engineer Corps is trying to dam it for no reason. The bog, all fifty thousand acres of it, is a living natural history of Kingdom County. It's a last bastion of Canada lynxes, pine martens, three-toed northern woodpeckers. It's home to six distinct subspecies of brook trout found nowhere else on Earth. Fugitive slaves hid here on their way to Canada. My own Abenaki ancestors hunted moose and bear here. Seven generations of Kinnesons have hunted and fished here. But even if they hadn't, wild places like the Great Northern Bog have their own right to exist."

"Mr. Kinneson, the Declaration of Independence stipulates that 'all men are endowed with the unalienable rights to life, liberty, and the pursuit of happiness.' I don't recall it mentioning that trout and wildcats and family hunting camps have the same rights."

"Thank you for raising that point, Justice O'Brien. Without unspoiled places like the Great Northern Bog to restore our humanness, our place in the natural world, we can't pursue our own happiness."

"Isn't that what national parks and national forests are for?"

"Absolutely. The entire Kingdom Gore would make a unique addition to our National Forest system. That's a great idea. Meantime, last slide."

Charlie clicked onto the shot of the log hunting and fishing camp with the yellow "condemned" notice on the door. He paused a little longer over the slide of the doomed camp. Then he said, "Family." Paused again but for the briefest moment before shutting off the projector. "Thank you, Justices. Lights, please."

On the evening of the day they'd visited the camp for the last time, a week after the Supreme Court ruled, along party lines and on the grounds of upholding the public good, for the engineer corp and against the Friends of the Bog, Charlie and Jim had supper together at the Common Hotel. Frannie and Athena had gone shopping in Littleton and wouldn't be home until later in the evening so the brothers had a couple of hours to kill. They sat at their usual table overlooking the disused railroad tracks and the village green. It was dusk now and spitting snow with heavy snow predicted to set in after midnight. That was to be expected in November in Kingdom County. The one commodity the Kingdom had a surplus of was snow.

Armand St. Onge Jr. had a good fire of fragrant maple splits crackling on the open hearth. On the birch-paneled walls of the barroom the mounted moose and deer and bear heads, the fishers and otters and the full-sized mount of the last catamount taken in Vermont, the trophy brook trout, many of which had been caught in the Great Northern Bog, gazed out over the dining room, which itself had something of the feel of a grand old sporting camp from a century ago.

"Okay," Charlie said. "Disclosure. Late yesterday afternoon I filed a stay of execution."

Jim looked at his brother.

"That's right," Charlie said. "Based on the discovery of a critical new piece of evidence. I've been poking around, doing some research. It seems, brother mine, that after our crazed ancestor 'Rebel Jim' was killed by federal troops in 1842, the Kingdom Republic never formally surrendered to Vermont or the United States. There was no Appomattox. Not a single resident was a signatory to the reincorporation of the Kingdom into the Union. Technically, Jim, the Kingdom isn't under the jurisdiction of the U. S. Supreme Court or any other court but its own. We're still an independent Republic. The Bog and the Gore still belong to the citizens of the Republic to hold for their descendants in perpetuity. Same way the village green belongs to the kids of Kingdom Common in perpetuity."

"You think they'll buy it? The court?"

"Of course not. Never in a million years. No stay of execution for us, bubba."

"Then why'd you bother to file it?"

Charlie thought for a minute. It was still early, they were the only diners. The only sound was the fire on the hearth.

"Jim, we Kinnesons have been getting our arses kicked up

here in the Kingdom for two hundred and fifty years. Why stop now? They've kilt us and they've whupt us and they've kicked our sorry arses from here to eternity. When's the last time we ever won anything?"

"So the court and the government, Washington, Montpelier, whatever, get the last word?"

"Oh, no they do not, my friend. They most assuredly do not get the last word."

"Then who does?"

Charlie pointed the neck of his empty straight across the table at Jim. "You do, Mr. Storywriter. Give 'em hell."

Then he raised the bottle over his head and waved it to get Armand St. Onge's attention. "Armand," he called out in his booming voice. "Bring me and this other man here two more cold ones."

9

What Pliny Knew

There was always a jolt of uneasiness involved in the sudden appearance of a hearse. This was the case even when you were expecting to see one, and this dawn, the Saturday before Easter Sunday 1900, Pliny had not been. This morning, standing on the parsonage porch behind the leafless bittersweet with last fall's bright orange berries still clinging to the vine and watching the mountain village of Kingdom Common come into resolution in the strengthening light, Pliny'd been daydreaming about the moment he'd fallen in love with Lake. That was the moment he'd first laid eyes on her, waltzing into the Great House ballroom at the Christmas jollification in that heartbreaking red dress, with a brimful glass of water balanced on her head. Swirling across the rosy white-oak parquet floor straight toward him—she had already set her cap for him though he had no way to know this at the time—to the wild strains of Fiddler John's "Arkansas Traveler" and never spilling a single drop. And then the abrupt sighting at the far south end of the common of that ebony dead wagon with its black-clad standing driver cracking the reins across the back of the galloping light-colored horse. Causing Pliny's next breath and the breath after that to come tighter. What the Reverend Doctor found most unsettling was the utter silence. The only noise was the steady hush of the High Falls on the river behind the parsonage. The oncoming hearse and running horse were as quiet as the mist rising off the common.

Now Pliny noticed that the horse's hooves were wrapped in black cloth, and the iron-rimmed wheels of the hearse as well. The driver had a short dark beard as uncompromising as a sexton's spade and shoulder-length white hair and wore a flowing dark mourning cloak and a top hat as rigid as a length of stovepipe. And stood with the reins in his black-gloved fist with a rigid upright probity as if he might be sheared from tin himself.

Only when the driver drew the rein and brought his steed to a skidding halt in front of the parsonage did the Reverend Dr. Pliny Templeton perceive that the animal had been painted. No, not painted. Whitewashed, though haphazardly, with its rich mahogany coat showing through the unevenly applied wash in ragged patches. Pliny knew this horse and the white-headed specter driving it.

From the coop behind the parsonage Pliny's red breeding rooster Charlie Kinneson III gave out a prolonged raucous cry audible at the far south end of the common.

"You, Reverend Templeton," the driver called out in a voice of brass. "Behold a pale horse."

Swiftly as some necromancer of yore the hearse driver produced from the folds of his sable cloak a horse pistol a good two feet long, which he leveled straight at Pliny's breast.

"Compose thyself, Africanus," roared the gunman. "Thine days in this world will come to an end ere the cock crows thrice tomorrow."

Of course he could run. Six passenger trains a day steamed south from the village of Kingdom Common in that era, four north. He could be in Boston by midafternoon. Montreal sooner. No. Pliny's running days were behind him. He was determined to run no more forever.

He could certainly defend himself from the madman. No one would blame him. But when the madman was also your deliverer from slavery and adoptive brother and closest friend in all the world? Unthinkable. Why, the pair of them ought to be out on the river together fishing the spring run of rainbow trout, vying for the largest fish, as they'd done these last fifty years for the biggest spring trout, first June peas, July sweet corn, August tomatoes: "Here's a basket of fresh-picked string beans, brother. I notice yours are yet to come into blossom. No doubt they'll overtake mine in the next fortnight."

But hold, Reverend Sidewhiskers. Today of all days is no time to derail yourself the way you did when you were teaching at your beloved Academy and your scholars tried to "get old Temp going" with one of his famous side stories.

"Tell how you and Charlie K stopped Pickett's barefoot boys at Get, Dr. T. Give us a bit of the rebel cry."

Was there ever a teacher who wasn't a born actor? Demur though he would, sooner or later he'd oblige them, and if the weather was warm, and the windows up, "Don't be alarmed," the villagers would reassure each other across the common at the post office and feed store, "that's just the old reverend demonstrating the rebel yell to his students over at the Academy."

Or longer ago still when he was just starting to preach and he'd deliver a Christmas homily at Easter or vice versa. The congregation would begin to exchange glances and try not to smile, as if to say, "There the old boy goes again, galloping off on one of his hobbyhorses." His design, of course, had been to deflect attention from his deeper heresies, in which, for a time, he had been successful.

But now it was time to walk down the length of the Common to the church for the short Holy Saturday service. If this was the end, as Charlie'd prophesied, then he would finish strong, as Charlie himself would have done in his place. He would end in a way his congregation would remember for a long time to come. He stopped briefly to pick up an empty Blue Seal Feed sack from the chicken house, then poked his head into the woodshed. He found what he wanted and headed down the village green to perform his office.

It was a plain country church of the Presbyterian denomination with no stained glass or paintings or graven images, and Pliny'd memorized the entire Easter weekend service long ago. Privately he'd never entirely understood why Jesus had been so set on going up to Jerusalem and tempting fate in the first place. Pliny supposed that he could chalk up Jesus' impatience to get on with matters to the fact that He was still young, just thirty-three. At least nobody could accuse him, Pliny, of acting rashly. Getting into his vestments in his study in the back of the church, he had no idea exactly what he'd say or how long it would take. It would take as long as it took. But now, dear Lord, there was the specter of his adoptive brother Charles Kinneson of the hearse and the galloping whitewashed horse, having manifested himself in the Kinneson family pew, producing his prayer book as he had for a thousand other services. He still wore his mourning cloak and, Pliny guessed, the horse pistol below it.

"Dearly beloved," Pliny began to the dozen congregants scattered through the pews. "I have a tale to tell you. A tale of death and of resurrection. But not perhaps the one you're expecting. Hark, now. Hear how I died for the second time on the day of my nineteenth birthday, and was resurrected that same day through my covenant with God."

"There was a man," Pliny began. "An ordinary man like any other save in one regard. This man was a slave, on a cotton plantation near Vicksburg, Mississippi. To make matters worse, he was also the illegitimate, half-white son of the plantation owner so that he grew up with one foot in the Great House, where he taught himself early on to read and write, and one in the Quarters. He was a neither-nor, betwixt-and-between creature from the outset. Indulged by his father, Judge Byrum Templeton. Despised by the judge's wife, Mistress Lucrezia, as a perpetual reminder of her husband's philandering. And, at best, tolerated by his brother and sister slaves.

"This slave was a good and faithful servant," Pliny continued from his pulpit. "He worked hard, became his father's right-hand man, and in the course of time married a beautiful and exceedingly clever slave girl from a neighboring plantation. She was a Creole woman and her name was Lake Ponchartrain. . . ."

What more now could he tell these maddeningly unimpassioned Yankees about the wild-hearted love of his life? That from the outset she made constant sport of him, as she seemed to of everyone and everything? The girl was a natural mimic and within moments of their first dance at that long-ago Christmas gathering she was clumping and left-footing it about the ballroom, taking him off ruthlessly.

From that evening forward he visited her at every opportunity. Rarely one to find himself at a loss for words, Pliny was tongue-tied around this beautiful and accomplished girl. She could cook to the taste of a gormandizer, entertain a brood of children of any age or color by the hour, build a fish trap, play the clavichord, and imitate to an uncanny degree the poor elderly unlettered Negro preacher who married them a month later in the little Negro church behind the Quarters. Nothing was safe from Lake's irreverence, especially the book by which Pliny would later earn his livelihood preaching from. Why, she wondered, didn't Adam break off a stout branch from the apple tree and kill the talking serpent? She wouldn't countenance any serpents, talking or otherwise, in her garden. Were there mules on Noah's ark? Where did he find them in the Holy Land? What did Jesus and the chosen twelve do for work? "Well, Miss Lake," she said in a deep voice like Pliny's, "you must understand that these are profound mysteries. It ain't—oh, dear, I mean it *isn't*—given to us to understand God's ways."

"She kept my feet on the ground," Pliny told his congregation. "I loved her beyond measure. Then she was sold down the river, to a notorious slave dealer named Smithfield, the very mention of whose name made Negroes from end to end of the Delta quake. Imagine, brothers and sisters. You go off to Vicksburg on business with your master. You return home only to discover that your bride of just a few months has been sold away by Mistress Lucrezia into heaven alone knows what unspeak-able species of bondage. Without hesitation the faithful servant went pelting off down the road, determined to offer himself up to Smithfield if only he could remain with Lake. 'Fetch my driving horse, Lady Ebony, and my gig and a long chain,' Mistress Lucrezia ordered. Straightaway the Lady and gig and chain were brought up. And with four burly field slaves on horseback in attendance, off she went after the fugitive, whom she ran to ground before he'd gone three miles.

" 'Now then, my dusky sir,' said Mistress. 'Since you wish to run, you shall have your fill of running.' She directed her attendants to affix one end of the chain to the rear axle of the gig and the other to the runaway's neck. Whereupon, she whipped Lady Ebony into a brisk trot, with the captured fugitive racing along behind for dear life. He fell, regained his feet, collapsed again. Sprawled out full length in the road. To prevent himself from strangling or having his neck broken he clung to the chain with both hands as Mistress dragged his torn body along the iron-hard road. Blinded by the dust raised by the horse and gig. Choking from the gritty dirt.

"Once home the mistress caused the good and faithful servant to be manacled by the wrist to a massive bolthead inside the furnace of a wrecked steamboat occasionally used by the judge as a makeshift jail. And ordered that, upon pain of sharing his fate, no one provide him with food or water until he tendered her his word that he wouldn't run again."

At this point in the story Pliny paused and surveyed the congregation. He wanted them to grasp the import of what he'd just said. That the word of the faithful servant was golden, no matter the circumstances. Out in the front pew Charles

Kinneson was nodding vigorously in agreement. Had his earlier incarnation as mad avenger been some sort of momentary insanity? Pliny knew that such things occasionally happened to the very old, nor was this the only time over the last half century he'd seen his deliverer and friend run amok. Or perhaps a joke? Hardly. His brother was not given to joking. Scripture reported a single instance of God laughing. Pliny doubted that Charles had laughed even once.

"There he was," the minister went on. "Alone. Sweltering. Bruised and cut. Parched. Chained to that great bolthead where the door of the steamboat's furnace had been blown off when the boiler exploded. And before he knew it the good and faithful servant was praying.

"'Mr. God,' he said. 'I know that it is not my place to horsetrade with you. But I know something else, as well. I know that which you joined together should not be put asunder. Therefore I wish to propose a covenant. I won't ask you to lead me to Lake. But if, gentleman sir, you will help me to free myself from this furnace, as you did Shadrach, Meshach, and Abednego, and take me under your protection while I search for her, I will be your good and faithful servant—kindly note that I don't say slave—and preach your word for the remainder of my days, be they long or be they short. Only let me search.'"

Once again Pliny regarded the congregation. It seemed to him that two or three late worshipers had ventured into the church since he'd started though he hadn't seen them arrive. That was how consumed he was by the story he was telling. As if he were asking not God, but his little Holy Saturday flock to grant him permission to look for his wife. The congregation was with him. He could tell from their upturned, expectant faces. They had to know, *had* to know what happened next, after the good servant made his supplication to God.

"What happened, good people, was what usually happens immediately after we pray. Exactly nothing. Wait. Don't mistake me. I do not say that prayer is unavailing. Not by a long shot. It is only that I have come to believe that it is God's intention that, whenever possible, we should look within and answer our prayers ourselves. And at just that moment, looking out in the johnsongrass and jimson weeds through the gash in the furnace where the door had been, the good servant espied the means of his deliverance."

Now, from behind the pulpit, Pliny produced the Blue Seal chicken-feed sack. From it he withdrew a double-headed splitting ax. "Aye, friends. Half concealed in the weeds lay a splitting ax with a broken-off handle. It was just within his reach, the snapped-off end of the handle lying beside it. From his shirttail the captive tore two strips of cloth. These he wrapped several times around his left forearm above his manacled wrist and the chain shackling him to the bolthead, tightening his makeshift tourniquet with the broken ax handle. Now there could be no hesitation. He must act this instant or he would never act at all.

In his right hand Pliny gripped the splitting ax just below its double blades. Made sure that every pair of eyes in the church was fixed on the axhead, which he brought down fast. Simultaneously, out from the sleeve of his ministerial robe shot his left arm. The sleeve fell away from his handless, padded left wrist. Of course his parishioners had always known he was missing a hand. Even knew he chopped it off himself, supposedly to free himself from slavery. In this regard the

parishioners had been mistaken. In fact he had maimed himself for life purely in order to search for his beloved Lake. His
freedom was incidental to his search.

"But wait," Pliny said. "If the good and faithful servant died
for the second time on the day his wife was sold down the river,
when did he die for the first time? Beloved, any of the millions
upon millions of men, women, and children ever held in bondage could answer that question. I, Pliny Templeton, died for
the first time on the day I was born into slavery. So endeth my
sermon on "Pliny Templeton's Covenant with God." The next
installment of my story will commence in half an hour. In the
meantime go forth, brothers and sisters, and spread the glad
tidings throughout the village. Come one, come all, to learn of
Pliny's resurrection."

"Down in the meadow, so far away,
Jack-in-the-pulpit's preaching today."
Hear "Pliny in the pulpit" preaching on
his life and times, Holy Saturday,
round the clock.

Some of the people Pliny'd been preaching to stood nearby,
gaping at the message he'd just put up on the letter board in
front of the church. Others seemed to be fanning out through
the town, as he'd exhorted them to, to drum up more business
for him.

"A stirring tale, brother." It was, dear God, Charles. "What
comes next, sir? You mentioned your resurrection?"

Pliny looked at his friend. Could this possibly be the same
fanatic who'd threatened his life at the parsonage an hour

before? Now Charles was encouraging him to tell his story to the town. Or some of it.

"Louisiana," Pliny said. "You remember Louisiana?"

"Aye," Charles said. "I do. Where I first heard you tell the story of your great covenant with God. And saw you fight. Louisiana."

"Aye," Pliny said. "Louisiana comes next."

"A slave gal? Name of Lake Ponchartrain? Talk French, read and write, tall with green eyes? No, suh. No such a gal pass through the market here at Natchez." Or Vicksburg, or Baton Rouge, or any of the plantations where he'd skulked up to the Quarters after dark to inquire. He traveled mainly by night in his own small blue fishing skiff, the left oar equipped with a jury-rigged leather harness to fit his wrist so he could row. It was hard to make the late-morning congregation, larger now, filling perhaps half of the church, see the big river because other than Charles Kinneson II few had ever seen a river anything like it. Not a river one quarter as large, one-tenth as dangerous. Under other circumstances it would have been the time of his life, dangers and all. How to make these stick-in-the-mud Vermonters understand?

"I traveled only by night for fear of being recaptured, and one thing I learned over the next two months was that the river was nearly as alive after dark as by daytime. Gar leaped out of the water and fell back with a splash like a plank dropped on the surface. Wild ducks clucked in their sleep. If I got too close a raft of them would fly up quacking as if the end of the world was at hand. And boats? Don't talk to me about boats, folks.

Keelboats freighting whiskey and lumber and grain downriver, red lanterns fore, green lanterns aft. Trotliners and flatboats. Ferryboats with sidewheels turned by horses or mules on treadmills. Scows and rafts and snag boats with winches and booms for pulling out sweepers and dismantling jams. Houseboats tethered to bankside trees in inlets and sloughs. Then of course there were the steamboats. Big as floating courthouses and lit up like Christmas and the waves from them lapping up on shore and giving out a long soft sigh as if they were happy to get there. You wanted to point the nose of your skiff directly into those waves. Otherwise they could tumble your boat backside over teakettle in less time than it takes to tell about it.

"I had to catch my breakfast, dinner, and supper out of the river, catfish mainly, and bream. Finding clear drinking water was a botheration. Once or twice I spied a cow in a pasture out of sight of the owner's house and had fresh milk. And the wild strawberries were coming on. Do you know how many wild strawberries it takes to fill up a man who's been rowing all night?

" 'Lake *Ponch*artrain? Ain't no Lake *Ponch*artrain round these parts.' Or, 'What you talking, boy? That the name of a big lake down Louisiane. Not no gal. What sort of name be that for a young gal? Probably sold off to the plantations in Brazil. Or put to work in a fancy house in Orleans. Get along now, 'fore us get in trouble consorting with you. Take this square of 'pone along. Got nothing else to give you. Go on now. Ain't no gal Lake here. Ain't no such a gal nowhere.'

"They would have known, of course, that there'd be a reward for me. They could have turned me in. They didn't. 'What you-all wants us to fix you for supper? Here, drat you

moonstruck cow eyes. Carry this flitch of bacon along. Man
can't live on love for a gone gal alone.' "

"Brother. Tell about President George Washington." Jesus
to Jesus and seven hands around! From his pew in the front of
the church, scant feet away, the madman was kibitzing. Actually kibitzing. Well, fine. Hadn't he always been at least half
crazed? At just eighteen Charles had taken it upon himself to
reroute the outlet of Lake Kingdom north instead of south,
stranding several mills just south of the Landing high and dry
on the original outlet with no waterpower, and at the same time
flooding out half the valley to the north, including the Common. There'd been talk of a tarring and feathering or worse so
Charles had skedaddled himself, gone South to "stir up the
darkies," as his enemies put it.

"New Orleans, good people, in that era, was the slave capi-
tal of the world, teeming with villainy of every stripe. Bull-
baiting, bear-baiting, raree shows, taverns by the score, ranks
of crooked brothels crowded elbow to elbow and leaning against
each other like barrelhouse drunkards trying to hold one another up. Sifting through the slave market and inquiring about
Smithfield and Lake, I made no progress in my search.

"In the meantime, I had made a mortal enemy myself. His
name was Dick Driver, and he was a multicolored parrot with
a scurrilous tongue who belonged to a New Orleans dandy and
boulevardier named Dave Dancer. Now this Dave Dancer had
trained his wicked familiar, upon sighting a man or woman of
color, to shower upon them the most opprobrious epithets. Dick
Driver was an abandoned parrot if one ever existed. He was
said to be over a century old and formerly the particular friend
and spiritual advisor of the infamous New Orleans buccaneer

Jean Lafitte. For some reason, this feathered paragon had taken an especial dislike to me.

"I would come around a corner and there they'd be, Dave Dancer, the man about town, who was no more nor less than a procurer for several of the better-known houses of ill repute, with the blasphemous parrot riding on his shoulder. 'Why,' said the bird to me, 'you sooty bastard, I'll have your liver for supper I will, I will. Son of Ham, son of Ham, son of Ham.' To this day, brethren and sisters, I believe that he knew exactly what he was saying.

"Yet working my way from brothel to brothel and patrolling the docks inquiring for Lake and the slave trader, Smithfield, garnering no information at all, I was beginning to think that neither my wife nor the slave dealer was in town. Surely if Smithfield had been there, he would have caught wind that I was looking for him and contrived to find me first.

"It occurred to me that if Lake had escaped from her captors, she might somehow have found her way back to her original home with the Ponchartrain family. I was told by a livery groomsman who styled himself a great jokester that they resided in a stately manse in the St. Charles arrondissement, with the family name embossed in gold filigree on the door. Imagine my dismay when, upon reaching the address I'd been given, I discovered that the trickster had directed me to the district cemetery. The "stately manse" was no more nor less than the Ponchartrain mausoleum.

"Not far away, in a little potter's field at the rear of the cemetery, where for generations the slaves belonging to the family had been laid to rest without the benefit of tombs or, I suspected, perhaps even coffins, was a small enclave of wooden tablets with the names of the deceased scratched into them. A few of these little wooden lozenges were draped with colored glass beads or bright scraps of cloth.

" 'Played out,' a squeaky voice behind me said. I whirled around to behold a spry manikin with a winking gold tooth. On his head sat a red, white, and blue showman's hat, nigh as tall as he was. Behind the dwarf was a handcart on which reposed two bundles, each about three feet long, wrapped in sailcloth. He was digging a shallow hole.

" 'Played out,' he said again. 'I mean the Ponchartrain family line. Played out from strong drink and opium and bankruptcy and duels, not to mention the yellow jack and malaria and syph and melancholia and a constitutional aversion to work of any kind whatsoever. That's *their* story, sojourner. What's yours?"

"I could not help smiling. 'I've no very unusual story,' I said.

The manikin, who was a very brash little manikin, wagged his finger at me as if he knew better. Then he looked solemnly at the bundles on the cart. There was a cholera epidemic sweeping through the city at the time so I inquired if the two deceased little ones belonged to him.

" 'Not little ones,' he said. "And not two. One. Here"— gesturing at the cart—"lies Jumping Jack Cantrell which was and is no more.'

"I expressed my condolences but said I could not help being curious. Was he not burying two bundles?

" 'Two bundles, one deceased,' he said. 'Severed.'

"With a final shake of his head over the sad fate of Jumping Jack, the dwarf turned his two halves into the hole, threw a few shovelfuls of dirt over them and told me to follow him and I would not be sorry I had. We wound our way back through the aboveground tombs, and along through the town toward the public gardens. There, near the river, a little off the main walkways and refreshment stands, we came to a pit in the ground with a few wooden poles over the top, to keep people from blundering into it, I supposed. Below lay a monstrous alligator a good fourteen or fifteen feet long. Its eyes, which were located in the top of its head, were fixed directly up at me.

"'Stranger, meet Father George Washington,' the little showman said.

"Drawing himself up to full attention, he snapped off a very trig salute to Father George. 'Mr. President, I have planted Jumping Jack who dodged when he should have shied. Here's his replacement.'

"The manikin turned back to me. 'Dollar a week and found, senator. You'll wrestle the commander in chief here catch-as-catch-can four times a day for the paying public. It's untaxing work. After a little lively snapping and scrapping, I'll toss George a bloody sheep's head. When he clamps onto it, spring at him and hold his jaws shut with your brawny forearms whilst I count to ten. You'll find it mere child's play. A gator, you see, has a bite down like a steam hammer but no strength at all to open its jaws. A babe in arms could hold a gator's mouth shut. Your star is on the rise, Rastus. This is your lucky day.'

"And that, brothers and sisters, is how the future minister of the First Presbyterian Church of Kingdom Common and founder and first headmaster of the Kingdom Academy, came to spend several months wrestling an alligator named for the father of our country, as a means of underwriting his ongoing search for his missing wife."

Pliny had neglected to bring his pocket watch. At twelve

o'clock the mill whistle would hoot out over the village to signal the noon break. He estimated that he had time before the
whistle blew to finish his Father George story.

"Now, folks, I must report that of all of the acquaintances I
made during my tenure in the netherworld of 'the Babylon of
the South,' as New Orleans was frequently referred to in that era,
young George was the most reliable. Oh, he took our matches
seriously enough, as you may be certain I did. But there wasn't
a speck of malice in the commander. From the outset, he and I
understood each other perfectly. We each had a job of work to
do. His was to eat me. Mine was to avoid being eaten. Now, I
will tell you one thing about these overgrown southern lizards.
As lethargic as they may appear to be when, say, they are
stretched out on a cypress log taking the sunshine of a mild
spring morning, they are, when they choose to be, as fast as a
quick-draw artist. You will see a fifteen-hundred-pound blur
hurtling your way and if, like my predecessor the unlucky
Jumping Jack, you miscalculate—I believe I need not elabo-
rate. I mean to cast no aspersions when I say that the species is
not clever. Ninety-nine times in one hundred a man will out-
think them. It's that one instance when you don't that skews
the equation. Recently, I'd had several all too close brushes
with the President's impressive dentition. I don't know whether
he was becoming smarter or I was growing careless. As a Presbyterian, I am not a betting man. Had I been, I would not have
placed odds on myself to last out the month. Therefore I decided to look for a more remunerative, not to mention a less haz-
ardous, line of employment.

"From the docks to Bourbon Street in that era there were
any number of enterprises requiring day laborers, but with only

one hand, I was somewhat restricted in what I could do for gainful labor. Still, there is always work for someone willing to do it. 'Mr. God,' I said one night after losing the tip of my left earlobe to the scaly commander that afternoon, 'I don't want you to suppose for a moment that I am repining. No, sir. We made an accord. You would allow me to search for Lake and I would go about your business and do your work. You've held up your end of the bargain. Now what I need is a real job. Don't mistake me. I don't mind earning my bread by the sweat of my brow. But I need a job where I won't keep forfeiting my essential components. That gator, bless his good soul, will soon have me whittled down to the small end of nothing if I keep this up.'

"As I've suggested, even the most modest of prayers isn't apt to take until you first follow the Master's good counsel to 'look within' for an answer. So I walked on down through the public gardens under the colored paper lanterns and past the orchestra and the stands selling sweetened ice and saltwater taffy and not far from the open market sat a small African Methodist church with live oaks along the plank sidewalk in front and a large azalea bush in blossom, all molten orange and red and copper, in the churchyard. And the bush was as incandescent as the bush consumed by holy fire out of which God delivered the commandments to Moses. And sitting around its base, in the shade of the oaks, were a few house slaves sent to do the marketing who had gathered here to eat their lunches and visit. I secured permission from the old Negro minister to stand on the church steps and preach as long as I shared the collection with him fifty-fifty. That seemed reasonable though I felt it only fair to caution him in advance that half of nothing was nothing. He laughed heartily and said he was glad to see that I had some humor in me because a preacher without humor was like a fish without gills or a bird without wings. But"—here Pliny fixed his gaze upon Charles II, in the front pew, who was nodding and leaning forward intently—"but a tall white man in a sober black suit and a black top hat, standing back a bit from the picnickers, frowned at me. Not, I thought, in disapprobation so much as puzzlement. Perhaps he was surprised to hear a black man speak with no trace of a Negro accent. He had pale blue eyes that seemed to pierce straight through me to a far-beyond bourn only he could make out. At the same time he seemed to see all there was to see about me. And there was about him, as well, a certain assessing aspect. As though he would weigh me in the balance and only then determine my mettle. It crossed my mind that he, too, might be a preacher."

Pliny smiled down at Charles II, who motioned to his adoptive brother to continue. Charles apparently had no objection to Pliny's telling this part of his tale.

So as he would narrate some sixty years later, two thousand miles to the north, from his pulpit in the Kingdom Common church, Pliny, fugitive slave, bereft of his wife, penniless, missing most of his left earlobe, stood on the top step of the church and began to tell, for the first time, the story of his covenant with God and his quest for Lake down the river to New Orleans. And asked the handful of house slaves if, using the wireless telegraph from Quarters to Quarters, they would help him in his search. Off in the distance, as the seeker spoke, he could hear the deep-throated African drums at the daily slave auction like the drumbeats of a Roman galley. And though he employed no Negro dialect, Pliny seemed to speak to the cadences of those drums from a far-flung shore.

When he was finished, and had showed them how he'd swopped off his own hand to search for the love of his life, he produced from his carpetbag, for a collection plate, a hard-used brass barber's basin that he had picked up for two bits from a pawn shop. Which came back to him as empty as it had gone out. The tall man in the frock coat now approached Pliny. "Handsomely done, Reverend," he said in a nasal twang as if he were suffering from a bad head cold. "You had your congregation, myself included, hanging on every word."

Pliny smiled at the gentleman and said, "Thank you, sir. I believe that I shall call it my 'Ten-Cent Sermon,' since ten cents is all I ever expect to earn from it." Pliny held the empty barber's basin out for him to see. "Today I did not fare that well."

The man in black replied, "Why sir, you preach as lively a sermon as any sky pilot between here and Boston-town. Where do you go now if I may inquire?"

"To the docks, I'm sorry to say," Pliny said. "To earn my bread in a very different manner. Preaching on a street corner won't buy my supper, I'm afraid."

At that moment in Pliny's narrative the furniture factory whistle, cattycorner across the Common behind the courthouse and Academy, gave a long, fluty blast. It was noon in Kingdom Common.

"One o'clock," Pliny said to his audience. "We recommence at one o'clock. Come one, come all. Bring a fellow parishioner or a friend. Come hear 'Pliny Boxes for His Bread on the Docks of New Orleans.'"

. . .

Linked arm in arm Charles accompanied Pliny up the village green through the chill sunshine of the Holy Saturday noon, the same route Charlie'd come in the ebony hearse pulled by the whitewashed horse that dawn. "A fine, manly talk, brother," Charles said. "How you wrestled the great leathery reptile and preached from the church steps. And they will love the bare-knuckle boxing to come. I think we understand each other now, thou and I. You will tell your tale up to the present. Only leaving out the boy."

"The truth is the truth."

"Aye, doctor. But surely you remember what sainted Augustine said on that score. We must never use it, I mean the truth, to harm anyone."

"It will harm no one at all, that I promise you."

They stopped in front of the parsonage. Pliny looking up at the porch through the orange bittersweet berries, in his mind's eye seeing himself as he was early that morning, looking down at the spectral hearse and its lunatic driver. How many hundreds of summer evenings, deep into the night, had the two of them sat out on that porch, thick as thieves, spinning tales, arguing religion—they could not argue politics because they were both good Lincoln Republicans—arguing fishing and hunting and literature. In winter they met alternate nights at one another's studies and read Boswell's *Life of Johnson* and Shakespeare's plays aloud to each other. And they'd gone through all of Dickens, Pliny's favorite author, and Miss Austen, Charlie's, though anyone who knew them might have thought it would be the other way around. For the last twelve years, since he was about six, the boy had joined them. Slipping in quietly and absorbing everything, as he did when the three of them went to the family hunting and fishing camp up on the border.

"You'll stop for a sandwich, brother," Pliny said. "A mug of cider."

"Aye, aye, we must recruit our spirit, mustn't we, brother, if we're going to see this through together?"

"This is nothing we need do together, Charles. It has only to do with me and the boy."

"You'll see what it has to do with me when more of the pious church fathers begin to filter in this afternoon and try to pull you down from the pulpit. I look forward to the moment, as I did our little counter-charge at Get. You remember, Pliny? How we stemmed the tide and turned back Pickett and his barefoot boys?"

Pliny, drily: "How could I forget?"

And Charles, as impervious to any kind of irony as to its near-cousin, humor: "Of course not, brother. It was a grand moment. Do you have some of that baked ham and sharp Vermont cheddar off the wheel left?"

"And a loaf of old Betsy Kittredge's homemade salt-rising bread."

"Then we'll feast, sir, and"—as Pliny poured the dark-amber cider—"to your health!"

"To yours," Pliny said to the man who, not eight hours earlier, had threatened his life. Then, "Where is the boy today?"

"He's fishing the run."

"And it still a month early."

"Do you think that will prevent him from catching what few fish may already be up?"

"I do not. I've promised him a silver cartwheel for every trout he takes over twenty-five inches."

And on in this vein.

Looking out from the pulpit some forty-five minutes later, Pliny was surprised to see the pews three-quarters full. Four of the church fathers sat grim-faced a few spaces down the front row from Charlie. Pliny conjectured that his adoptive brother had been right. Sooner or later, probably sooner, they would try to stop him. Charles was clearly looking forward to that moment.

"Along the river," Pliny began, "perhaps a mile away from the Negro church where I'd preached, was a string of warehouses where ships were loaded and unloaded. Here we spotted some men, singly and in pairs and small groups, slinking down a lane between two windowless storage buildings. My new companion, who had introduced himself as Charles Kinneson, a Yankee-man from New England, and I followed them, into an inner courtyard. Here two over-sized bruisers, stripped to the waist with their suspenders dangling, were preparing to fight. Other men were circulating through a crowd of one hundred or so spectators, taking wagers. When the bets were in, the pugilists put up their hands and, with a roar from the wicked onlookers, clashed together. I could see immediately that neither of these brutes had been trained in the Marquis of Queensberry's School of Fisticuffs but they whaled away at each other with goodwill until at last one went down and did not get up. The winner stolidly returned to wait for another opponent outside the makeshift circle of sawdust and dirt that served as a ring.

"Next a fellow with bright green galluses, a hairy chest, and hair growing well down onto his forehead sprang into the ring, turning a somersault in midair like an ape. 'Who'll go up against Baboon Bob?' a jim-dandy man collecting bets called out. Bob, in the meantime, pranced around in the ring, tossing cartwheels and shadowboxing. No one seemed eager to enter into combat with him.

" 'Do you bet, sir?' my new friend said.

" 'If I had the funds, sir, I would accept Baboon Bob's challenge and administer a bit of instruction to him or to any of these plug-uglies.'

" 'Did you box, then, before your mishap?' He nodded at my handless, leather-padded wrist.

"I smiled. 'It is not that, sir, that prevents me from entering the lists. I grew up boxing in my father's Quarters. Not to put too fine a point upon matters, I have not one cent to my name.'

"Charles Kinneson looked at me thoughtfully. From a snap purse in his side trouser pocket he produced a double eagle, which he pressed into my hand. 'My old Scotch beliefs prevent me from casting a wager,' he said. 'Go ahead, friend, and bet on yourself. If you win, keep your winnings. If you lose, you owe me nothing.'

"As Baboon Bob continued his capers, I held up the double eagle. 'Gentlemen. I have here two pretty yellow birds that say I can knock Bob senseless in ten seconds flat.'

"The jim-dandy took my coin. 'Name?'

" 'Reverend Cannonball,' I said, tipping a wink to my new friend.

"Oh,' said the impresario. 'A jackleg nigger preacher. Bob will make short work of you.'

"There was some further betting in the crowd, not much, because only a few gamblers were willing to wager that a one-handed preacher could beat Baboon Bob, who was now milling his fists over his head and howling.

"I stepped into the ring. The triangle rang out and Bob came charging. He hurled himself into a handspring in order to come down upon me feetfirst. Having anticipated some such simian antics, I turned sideways and administered such a rap to his crown with my good hand that he collapsed at my feet and lay there still as a babe in arms. The triangle went to signify my victory."

Pliny paused, smiled, pointed out the church window at the longtime rival Baptist church next door. *A minister without a sense of humor was like a fish without gills or a bird without wings.* "Later," he said, "I heard that Bob's match with me was the last of his bare-knuckle career. He went on to become a Baptist preacher, specializing in talking in tongues."

Now Pliny hesitated again. He would have to telescope much of what happened next in order to tell what he needed to by Easter dawn. He could not squeeze in everything.

After the boxing match, he and his new backer strolled down Bourbon Street, and Pliny told him about his search for the slave dealer Smithfield and Lake. Charles listened without interruption except once to mutter fiercely, in his harsh Yankee twang, the words "slavery" and "abomination." Ahead, beside a public watering trough for horses and mules, stood a bootblack's chair. Pliny was still heated from his boxing match so, dipping the former barber's basin into the burbling trough, he drenched his head with the cool water, then repeated the process. Charles asked if he could examine the basin. He turned it over two or three times in his hands, then said to the boot-black, a boy of twelve or thirteen who'd been watching them, "I would like to rent your chair, lad, for ten minutes or so," and flipped him a dollar. Then, beckoning at the tall stand, "Sit ye, sit ye, Pliny. Ascend the rude throne."

Pliny had never had his boots blacked by another man nor did he intend to impose such a servile task on a member of his own species—even a Yankee—now. But Charles said nay, nay, sit down, he had something quite different in mind. Most reluctantly, Pliny got up in the chair while Kinneson filled the basin with water from the trough. Over Pliny's laughing protest he then proceeded to kneel, whisk off Pliny's boots and stockings, and *wash his feet.*

These ablutions concluded, Charles fell to drying off Pliny's feet with the skirts of his frock coat. In the meantime who should come lollygagging down the street but the insufferable boulevardier Dave Dancer and, on his shoulder, his execrable parrot Dick Driver.

"Nigger, nigger, chain him up," the bird shouted out.

Dave Dancer reproved Kinneson as follows: "What, sir, can you be thinking, to wash a nigger's feet? Give over that blasphemy this instant."

"Burn he, cut he, hang he high. Hang dat nigger out to dry," screamed the parrot.

Kinneson stood up. Quite casually he reached out, wrung the parrot's neck, and threw the carcass into the cobbled street. Dave Dancer gave out a shrill cry and made a cut at Kinneson with his gold-knobbed walking stick. Kinneson parried aside the intended blow, swooped Dancer over his head and flung him into the horse trough.

"I don't know about you, friend," Kinneson said, "but I am as sharp set as a spring she-bear just out of her den. Let us stop at the next chophouse."

Some of these goings-on Pliny summarized for the congregation, far to the north, on that fair-and-foul Holy Saturday afternoon of April clouds and sun showers more showery than sunny. Some of the most peculiar happenings—the foot washing—he saw no reason to bring up. Surely it was just a matter of time before the astonished church fathers would rise as a body to usher him away from their pulpit, out of their church once and for all. Pliny could see Charles watching them out of the tail of his eye. As long as Pliny did not bring up the boy, Charles would see to it that he could speak his piece.

Over chops and mugs of beer—Kinneson said his religion forbade the use of strong spirits but nowhere did the tenets of his old Presbyterianism proscribe a cooling tankard of beer or ale—he told Pliny something of his own history. He said he was born and raised in northernmost Vermont, the son and grandson of abolitionist newspapermen and whiskey distillers. Several years ago he had been compelled to "leave Vermont in some haste." Pliny smiled. Kinneson shook his head. "No, Pliny, you mistake me. My sudden departure involved no member of the fairer sex, but rather a little geological misapprehension. A little matter of rerouting the outlet of a local pond to help power the family distillery, with just a bit of temporary flooding in the valley below. Suffice to say I wandered South, sending home dispatches on the horrors of slavery, which were widely reprinted in abolitionist gazettes throughout the North. To do this I traveled incognito, often using false names and forged papers."

When Kinneson's talk turned to slavery he underwent a transformation. His pale eyes seemed illuminated by an interior light. His lean body began to sway and he nodded to himself as his eyes looked off toward that faraway place only he could see. He confided to Pliny that, while he probably could have safely returned to Vermont a year ago without much fear of retribution, he had stayed on in the South on "a very private enterprise of a 'railroading nature,'" for a group of northern clergymen, politicos, and newspaper editors, to which he and his father had long belonged. Pliny knew immediately that he was speaking of the Underground Railroad, by which fugitive slaves were spirited north to free states and Canada, and that by coming to New Orleans, Kinneson was risking his life, as Pliny was his own.

"Now, Pliny," Kinneson continued after looking around the chophouse to make sure he was not being overheard. "You may be surprised to learn that I have had my eye on you for some time. Word travels fast, you know. When I heard, through certain connections I have at the slave market, that you were making inquiries concerning the whereabouts of a slave dealer named Smithfield, my ears pricked up. I too have an interest in locating Satan Smithfield. He is, let us say, at the head of a list of southern businessmen whom I am most eager to call upon before returning home. Let me show you my letter of introduction to these entrepreneurs."

Kinneson made a quarter-turn in his chair and nonchalantly brushed back his frockcoat so that, for a fleeting moment, Pliny glimpsed a long, deadly-looking pistol holstered at his waist. "I have paid my compliments to several of these men already. I fear, however, that our Mr. Smithfield has slipped through my fingers. Our fingers, Pliny. Yours and mine. I know you seek him also. As a means to finding your wife. I take it you have made no headway in that regard?"

Pliny told the man who was soon to become his deliverer that though he had made no progress in discovering the whereabouts of either Lake or Smithfield, he believed that he had perhaps eliminated some possibilities. "I don't think she's in Vicksburg or Natchez. Nor does it seem that she is here in New Orleans. Friend, I dread the worst. That she is mewed up in some backcountry redoubt across the river deep in the Territories. Or worse yet that she has been shipped to the Brazilian coffee plantations. I understand that, like you, I place my life at greater risk every day I inquire for Smithfield. But only he can tell me Lake's fate."

When Pliny concluded his tale Charles Kinneson was silent for a time. Finally he said, "Pliny, I have some reason to believe that if Smithfield was in New Orleans, he has now hit north again. He has been known, if the remuneration is adequate, to travel clear to Canada to capture and return a fugitive slave, or even to kill runaways in order to set examples. He is suspected in the murder of two of my own business associates in the North, both of them prominent in the 'rail' company. I believe, however, that there is a way to lure him to Vermont. We will do so on the pretext of offering a large reward for your capture. Once there, we will take him and, before putting him on trial for the murder and enslavement of Negroes, extract from him by whatever means are necessary the fate and whereabouts of your beloved Lake."

Pliny replied that he had deep misgivings about using un-

Christian methods to acquire the information he sought. Could they not, he wondered, once they had captured Smithfield, offer to spare his life in return for Lake's location? They could not, Kinneson replied. He would handle all necessary transactions with Smithfield himself. Other than acting as bait to lure the demon north, Pliny need have no further part in the scheme.

Kinneson then stood up and poured a little beer from his tankard into Pliny's collection plate. He placed his hand on Pliny's brow and proclaimed, to the utter consternation of their fellow diners, "Lord, I beseech thee to make this good man, Pliny Templeton, an instrument of thy will."

He dipped his fingers into the basin and sprinkled the beer onto Pliny's forehead and said, "Pliny, I baptize thee in the name of Our Merciful All-loving Savior, Jesus Christ, to make you the instrument of the Lord God Jehovah in bringing Satan Smithfield to justice. His will be done, His Kingdom come. I now pronounce you, Pliny Templeton, His instrument and Angel of Retribution for all your remaining days."

A man at an adjacent table gave out a guffaw and said he much doubted that the Lord would soon be making any black nigger His instrument. So fast that Pliny could scarcely follow his movements, Kinneson had his pistol out of his waistband and up against the man's temple. "You said?"

"Nothing," the lout replied. "I said nothing."

"Quite right," Kinneson said. Laying the two-foot-long weapon on the table where he could instantly seize it up again, he congratulated Pliny on his baptism.

"Sir," said Pliny, "to humbly serve the Lord all my days as His minister is my design. As you know from hearing my sermon, I've made my own covenant with Him to do so. But I can be no such tool of his vengeance. Indeed, my own faith comes and goes with the weather. I lay no claim to godliness."

"Minister, your honest doubt is proof of your faith. Was it not old Aquinas who said that doubt inheres in all true faith? The Christ Himself faltered briefly and remonstrated with His Father for forsaking Him on the cross."

Smiling in a genial way, "Tell me, Pliny. What is it you wish for most?"

"To find my wife."

"You shall do so. Here is my hand upon it."

Kinneson clasped Pliny's hand in his two and it was like inserting it between two millstones. "Now, what do you wish for next?"

"Freedom for both Lake and myself."

"That too you shall have. Let us shake again."

Rather warily this time, Pliny extended his hand and again Kinneson bid fair to crush it between those two grindstones.

"Now, minister. Ask me for one more boon. For you're putting your life at risk for me."

"Knowledge," Pliny said.

"Ah. You shall have that, too. You shall have all the knowledge you desire. In the meantime, earlier today I took the liberty of booking passage for both you and myself on the packet *Belle of Savannah*, bound for New York in the morning. There we will rendezvous with my dear friend and colleague, Mr. J. B., to lay plans to lure Smithfield north and deal with him as I have described. Then, before you begin your formal education, you and Mr. J. B. and I will return south and purchase or, by other expedients, emancipate your beloved wife and bring her north. Are you for it?"

"I am."

This time Charles Kinneson did not put out his hand but rather stepped around the table and clasped Pliny in a bear hug like a brother, which is how Charles would address him hence-forward. As soon as Pliny could catch his breath he said, "If I may ask, sir, who is your colleague Mr. J. B.?"

"Brother, he is soon to become the Moses of your people," Kinneson replied. "His name is John Brown and he is the greatest man I have ever known."

So the afternoon came and wore away as Pliny nattered on from the pulpit, now with one side story after another, and even the church fathers seemed at times to be swept along by his tales. Charles II and his crony Brown shot and killed Smithfield upon sight on the day he arrived in Kingdom County, posing as a missionary with a magic lantern show. Charlie'd claimed he meant only to wing the slave catcher. Pliny had no choice but to believe him. Charles kept his word by sending his adoptive brother first to the state university and then Princeton Theological Seminary, Pliny graduating from both institutions with the highest honors. This part of his history was well-known in Kingdom Common, as was the fact that he ministered for several years, with great popularity, at the Church of New Canaan, the granite-mining town twelve miles north of the Common, founded by fugitive slaves, before being recruited for a vacancy in the pulpit of the Presbyterian Church in the Common.

"Where," Pliny said now—oh, he still knew how to hold an audience—"if I never did anything quite right in the eyes of my beloved congregation, I never did anything wrong enough to get myself sent down the road." Laughter.

He'd needed all his humor, and all of his extraordinary energy as well, when he began teaching and headmastering at the Academy he and Charles had built almost entirely by themselves next to the courthouse. A good enough minister but a great teacher, they'd said of him. And what, Pliny inquired of his congregation, was a great teacher anyway but a failed minister? More laughter.

The clock in the steeple of the Baptist church next door chimed six. Why hadn't Pliny noticed it striking out the hours until now?

"Suppertime," he said to his now nearly full house. "Seven o'clock sharp. Be here. My text will be 'What Pliny Knew.'"

It was this simple. He would continue to return south to search for Lake for the rest of his life. In the war he served as regimental chaplain to Col. Charles "Mad Charlie" Kinneson's Vermont Second. Later he and Charles escaped from Andersonville by feigning their own deaths. During Reconstruction—a misnomer if there ever were one when it came to the recently emancipated slaves, who'd had nothing to reconstruct—with Charles's financial backing, he'd built more than one hundred "Templeton Schools" to teach reading and writing to Negroes throughout the former Confederacy. He would never find Lake. False sightings were the hardest. And charlatans scheming to cheat him out of the handsome reward he advertised in Negro newspapers. At first more than a few young widows and grass widows and even some of the young unmarried women in his congregation set their caps for him. As they came to understand that, never mind in the eyes of God, he still regarded himself as married and always would, they mothered him instead of courting him. He supposed the girl, Charlie's red-headed firebrand daughter Mary, Queen of Scots, reminded him of Lake. Her anarchic ways, her quarrel with the stern old Presbyterian God of Abraham and Isaac and Jacob, her precocious womanliness at seventeen. Exactly who seduced whom was immaterial. He was forty years her senior and had abused the trust of his profession and his dearest friend. Her father and mother, the Charles Kinnesons, adopted the boy. Mary removed herself to New Canaan, locally known as Niggerville, and died along with one hundred others when the Vermont Klan burned them alive in their church. Charlie swore a great oath on Brown's sword, Pottawattomie, which he inherited from his abolitionist colleague after Harper's Ferry, to hunt down and slay each of the twenty young and not-so-young local Klansmen who'd ridden on New Canaan. He made good on his oath. Young James, supposing his grandfather Kinneson to be his father, Pliny his reverend preceptor but no more, flourished under the loving guidance of two fathers. Pliny taught him and a select handful of upper-form students Greek and Latin, taught him the names of all the birds, animals, plants, minerals of the Kingdom. Taught him baseball. The boy, a lefty, becoming the best pitcher in the history of the Academy. Charles, likewise his wife, indulged James in the adoring manner of any grandparents, which was a splendid way for him to grow up. Charles and Pliny never went to the woods or much of anyplace else without him. He had red hair and blue eyes like his birth mother and a devilish smile and his birth father's wit. Of all of Pliny's students, he was most expert at "getting old Temp going."

Over a cloth-covered basket of fried chicken, baked potatoes, coleslaw, and maple sugar pie provided by Charles's wife, and two mugs apiece of hard cider from Charles's Westfield-Seek-No-Furthers:

"Brother," said Pliny. "Walk not a mile but a mere hundred feet in my shoes. The boy must know who he is. He and his— our—descendants who they are. And yes, the all-knowing Common must know, too."

"Hoot, Pliny. You just want to take credit for him."

"What if I do? Who wouldn't? Why do you oppose it? Don't you have faith in him to handle it?"

"Pliny, Pliny, my dear beloved brother. Of course I do. It's the village I don't have faith in. And the great spinning world beyond. Not the boy. I have complete faith in the boy. Now and forever."

"Hasn't the village and the world too since I wrote my strange *Ecclesiastical History of Kingdom County* handled me well enough? There's talk of establishing a scholarship in my name at the university."

"Aye. Now that it suits them to do it. Pliny, I cannot allow it. You must end your wonder-story before the boy arrived on the stage."

"Know then that I have already written to him. He and no one else will see this letter. If for some reason I should not be extant to tell him."

There was a tremendous knocking on the parsonage door. "Minister, come out. Come out, instantly."

Six or seven church fathers in their Sunday frock coats stood on the porch. A throng with pine torches in the street nearby, curiosity seekers. A shot rang out from Charles's pistol, directly beside Pliny's ear.

"Back," Charles roared. "Back, dogs. I'll shoot the first cur to stand in our way. The Reverend shall finish his tale if he wishes."

But to Pliny, "Pray don't, brother. Do not quite finish it. Do not. I know you think me prideful. I know you think me hasty. Are you not more prideful and hasty yet? What possible good can come of such a revelation?"

"This has nothing to do with pride or haste. It has to do with the truth."

"Pliny, come. Let me make one more attempt to reason with you. This is about your beloved Lake, is it not? You looked hard and hard for sixty years but never found a trace. Do you feel somewhat of the same loss with the boy? Because he has never known who you truly are? Pliny, he could scarcely love you more did he know. Perhaps he already does, or suspects. Save for his red topknot and blue eyes there is the strongest resemblance between you two. Who knows what the boy knows? Leave it be."

"If he suspects, that's all the more reason to tell him."

"And do you intend to tell him how his mother's murderers, the Klansmen, died? At my hands? That his grandfather, whom he supposes to be his father, ran mad and slaughtered twenty people? Murderers though they were? I say again, Pliny, leave it be. None of this can make up for losing Lake. That's my fault. Take my weapon and here on the parsonage steps redress that terrible crime, my crime, of killing Smithfield before we could interrogate him."

"Brother, my mind is made up. Look. Someone's lighted the church. If this is to be our last walk together, let us then make it together."

And they did, down the Common, arm in arm. It was markedly colder now. They might wake up to snow on Easter morning.

The heroics of Col. Charles Kinneson's Second Vermont Regiment, who turned away Pickett's charge at Gettysburg and thereby in one short July afternoon turned the tide of the battle and the war for the Union, were well-known and much-celebrated in the village. Though of course the myth of "Mad Charlie's" one-man countercharge and the facts of what happened that miasmic afternoon in the green hills of Pennsylvania were as different as noon and darkest midnight. In his narrative that Easter eve in 1900, Pliny cleaved to the conventional story without exactly distorting what actually happened. Meade's orders had been clear. The regiment would wait until Pickett's men were within five rods, then open with grape and chain, and only after that mount the flanking charge. Such was not Charles's style. Without notice he gave out a great piercing ululation as if in response to the Johnnies' own fearsome outcry and started down the hill, waving Brown's sword like an avenging blue angel. Pliny tackled him just in time to drive them both to the ground inches under the canister from the hilltop above, screaming like ten thousand deadly steel hornets. Charles leaped to his feet, and with Brown's sword fought off the swarming rebels who'd survived the first cannonade, continued swinging the sword while by main force Pliny dragged his friend and commander back up the hill before the second roaring fusillade that actually won the day for the Union. Charlie thrashing and resisting. Clearly wanting to die a martyr. Meade gave him a button cut from his uniform jacket, then later a medal of honor.

"Give us a taste of the old rebel yell, Dr. T."

Pliny hadn't seen the boy come into the packed church, but he'd know his voice anywhere. There he was, standing beside Charles, in the first pew of the room, in his rubber knee boots, whipcord trousers, and red flannel shirt, like a young jack on the log drives that still came down the river each spring. The boy had already proven his own manhood the year before, at sixteen, by riding a saw-log over the falls and down through the rapids below which both Charles and Pliny had strictly forbidden him to do. That thick mop of red-gold Kinneson hair, those bold blue humorous eyes. And holding out from his waist, one in each hand, their broad tails brushing the worn old maple flooring of the church, their crimson side bands glowing like liturgical robes in the lantern light, two gigantic rainbow trout.

Pliny grinned, dug in his vest for two cartwheels, and spun them out in the lantern light, the boy plucking them out of the air deftly as Honus Wagner, one, two, without thinking. That's how sure-handed he was.

"Nay, son," Pliny said. He'd begun calling James "son" some years ago, and Charles hadn't objected. "Sit. Join us with your two fine fishes. But first hold them up for the people to see."

The boy grinned and displayed the fish to the congregation. Pliny's eyes brimmed with pride as James wedged himself into the pew between Charles and the church fathers, who were looking askance at the fish as if they'd been conjured from some Arthurian legend. Pliny soldiered on with his tale. Charlie had been captured pursuing Lee's retreating forces with a ragtag handful of Green Mountain Boys, Pliny trying futilely to rescue him. He'd written an entire chapter in his fabled *History* about their months at Andersonville so was able to pass over that briefly. It was Charlie who'd organized the prisoners into divisions and companies and been both commanding officer and father to them while Pliny saw to their spiritual needs.

Baseball. Oh, yes, baseball! Pliny'd brought the game back to the Kingdom after the war, cut out the first diamond in New England at the south end of the Common, played with gusto and élan himself. He'd been known in those years as "Baseball Pliny." Why, with his swift one-handed swing he'd once clouted a ball off the upper façade of the brick shopping block across the street from— "Show us, show us Dr. T," the boy called out, his blue eyes sparkling with mischief and delight, like his mother's, like Lake's for that matter. And the glorious rivalries with Prof. Cyrus Barton's crew from the Landing: "We fought John Reb at Get and the Wilderness but never with quite the righteous hometown fervor of those cross-county contests." The *smack, smack, smack* of James's rifling fastball, accurate as a sniper's ball, cracking in Pliny's pancake-thin three-fingered glove evening after evening on the Common. The sudden dip of his yellow hammer twelve-to-six curveball. Unhittable.

Reconstruction. By Reconstruction there were agencies, in Memphis, Atlanta, New Orleans, and elsewhere, agencies designed to reunite families torn apart by slavery and the war and the anarchic aftermath. Pliny availed himself of them all, all to no avail. It was as though the day she'd been sold down the river with Smithfield, Lake had disappeared from the face of the earth. Maybe Pliny talked more, that Easter eve, about all this than he'd meant to. The steeple clock next door tolled midnight. Resurrection day. People overflowed into the church vestibule to hear what he said. To tease Charles, James had slung his two great fishes onto the old man's lap to hold like sleeping toddlers. Charles shook his head and nearly smiled. He did not push the fish away.

Like many another scholar, Pliny was slightly absent-minded. What was it Lake said when he misplaced a pen or a collar? "Look for it where you lost it, boy. You lose your head if it wasn't attached." He went back once, twice, three times to the ruined empty plantation where he'd grown up near Natchez, the bastard son of the owner and a slave woman. There was nothing left to trace. Charles, by now a very wealthy man from manufacturing and selling the whiskey his religion forbade him to consume, spared no expense to assist in the search, which became a mission, then quickly a quest, not for a grail but a girl who, of course, was no longer a girl but, if still alive, well into her middle years.

At last, in the remaining few hours before dawn, the church began to empty out. Even some of the church fathers had gone home. Pliny spoke of his teaching years back at the Academy after Reconstruction as some of the happiest times of his life since losing Lake. And what a teacher he was. He taught his students to cook. Once a week a class would put on a dinner for the rest of the students. Pliny told them no one who could cook would ever be out of a job and cooking was fun besides.

With Pliny, learning and teaching were always fun. He was becoming a myth himself.

Off in the east a faint strip of pink, not unlike the color, now fading fast, of the two trout in Charles's lap. Pliny walked to the back of the church and opened the door. A minute went by. Maybe two. Then from the far end of the village, the shattering *cock-a-doodle-doo* of Charles Kinneson III, Pliny's rooster.

"Are you finished, Reverend? With your marvelous tale?"

Pliny wasn't sure who'd asked the question. Not Charles. "Not quite," he said. "Not quite."

He left the church door open though it was much colder now and spitting snow.

Pliny remounted the preacher's dais but not the pulpit. He stood on the edge of the dais, six feet from Charles and the boy. He looked at the dwindled congregation. "There was a girl," he said. "Not Lake."

The rooster crowed again. Charles handed the fish back to James, almost tenderly. He stood.

"Reverend," he said. He was weeping.

Pliny had never seen his adoptive brother weep.

The rooster crowed again.

Resolutely, Pliny continued. His voice was strong. His smile, at the boy, and at Charles, nothing but kind.

"Red-haired," he said. "Brilliant. Beautiful. Free-spirited. Her too, I loved. Not in the way I'd loved and still love my Lake. But I loved her."

The shot reverberated in the church like a cannon. Pliny dropped to the floor. The cock crowed for the third time and the sky to the east turned as red as Gettysburg. It was Easter morning in Kingdom Common.

10

The Songbirds of Vermont

Ruth Kinneson woke up worrying about bluebirds. When she'd first come to the Kingdom, more than three-quarters of a century ago, the bluebirds had no trouble finding hollow wooden fence posts or cavities in old apple trees to nest in. Nowadays no one used wooden fence posts, and home apple orchards were much less common. Occasionally in the early spring bluebirds stopped by to inspect the birdhouses Jim and Frannie had put up. Then they moved along elsewhere. Recently it seemed to Ruth that songbirds in general were diminishing in number in Vermont. She hadn't seen a bobolink or a meadowlark yet this summer. Ruth had written about their absence in her weekly nature column in *The Monitor*, though why she'd wake up fretting about the birds on today of all days was as much a mystery to her as how she'd gotten to be ancient in the first place.

This much was certain. At 102, Ruth Kinneson was the oldest living resident of Kingdom Common with a mailing address outside the village cemetery. "Living" because if you counted the Reverend Dr. Pliny Templeton, he had her beaten hands-down. Today Pliny would turn 200. And yet, Ruth thought as she began to get washed up for the day ahead, Pliny could probably hang from his pole in the former science room of the Academy, gazing down at the village below, for another century or two and still not be considered a real Vermonter, much less a Commoner. Ruth could relate to that. She'd been born and raised in Boston and was a Kinneson by marriage only.

Like Pliny in his day, Ruth wore several hats. Her day job was village librarian and curator of the county historical museum. Besides her nature column, she wrote monthly essays for *The Monitor* on new books the library'd received and on local historical topics. She was organist at the United Church, tutored adult-ed students, helped high school kids research their term papers, ran a women's book club, and maintained a garden large enough, as her elder son Judge Charlie Kinneson said, to feed the Army of the Potomac. Ruth liked to tell her family that the fact that she'd never stopped working, combined with her daily walks to and from the Common, accounted for her becoming a centenarian.

Today Ruth wore an elegant white summer dress that her daughters-in-law, Dr. Frannie Lafleur Kinneson and principal Athena Allen Kinneson, had given her for her 102nd birthday. She slipped a matching pair of low heels into a plastic bag to wear at work, finished her bowl of oatmeal, and checked herself out in the dressing-table mirror in her bedroom. Her blue eyes were as interested and amused—amused at herself, as often as not—as ever. Neither her tawny blonde hair nor her complexion had faded much. She still had her figure though she'd had a brush with breast cancer twenty years ago. Her teeth were excellent and she was unabashedly vain about them.

Back in the kitchen, through the empty stovepipe hole in the wall between her side of the farmhouse and Frannie and Jim's, Ruth heard Frannie say, "Where's Mom, sweetie? Has she left yet?"

"I think so," Jimmy said.

Their voices sounded as though they were sitting at Ruth's kitchen table. The stovepipe hole had astonishing acoustical properties, both relaying conversations from one side of the house to the other and amplifying them. Ruth, the first Kinneson to become computer literate, referred to the hole in the wall as the family iPod.

In fact, there was a double wall between Ruth's kitchen and Jim and Frannie's, with a dead space about three feet wide between the two partitions. Family lore held that there had once been a secret door into the cubbyhole where fugitive slaves on the Underground Railroad had been hidden before making the last leg of their flight to Canada, ten miles north of the Kinneson farm. In 1812, led by James Kinneson I, Kingdom County had seceded from the Union over the issue of slavery. For the next thirty years the Kingdom had maintained its independence as a free republic, raising its own militia, writing its own constitution, and establishing a sanctuary for runaway slaves on the nearby border. Ruth often wondered. Would she, like her husband's abolitionist ancestors, have had the courage to defy the Fugitive Slave Act and assist runaway families on their way north? She hoped so. Ruth's older son, Judge Charlie Kinneson, said that the hidey-hole between the walls had probably been created to stash booze during Prohibition. Jimmy tended to agree with his brother since, as the Reverend Dr. Pliny Templeton himself had pointed out in his *Ecclesiastical, Natural, Political, and Social History of Kingdom County*, in the Kingdom Republic the Underground Railroad ran aboveground. Slave catchers who ventured there disappeared. The Reverend Dr. Templeton was a fugitive slave himself. Whatever purpose the hidey-hole between the partitions might have served, Ruth loved the lore connected with it. Ultimately, the secret space was as mysterious to her as her own longevity.

Ruth couldn't help wondering, as she headed out through the sweet-smelling woodshed into the summer dawn, what earthly purpose there could be in living so long. Making her way down the lane along the river where seven generations of Kinnesons had fished for their beloved brook trout, Ruth catalogued in her mind, for her weekly nature column, the July wildflowers along the bank. Paintbrush. Vetch. Daisies. Black-eyed Susans. A lone cardinal flower on a rocky islet in the river. On the other side of the lane, the pasture where Gramp had once grazed his Jerseys, was overrun with meadowsweet. Ruth loved this waist-high woody shrub that seemed to colonize abandoned fields and pastures overnight. Later this month it would put out tiny white petals splashed with raspberry-colored streaks. But once meadowsweet established itself, its tangled aggressive roots were hell to clear out of a field. Unlike many other invasive nuisance plants that had overrun Kingdom County in recent decades—Japanese bamboo, phragmites, purple loosestrife—meadowsweet was native to northern Vermont. Like the Kinnesons, it was troublesome and enduring.

As Ruth crossed the single-lane red iron bridge to the paved county road, a male oriole flushed from the willows along the bridge pool. Ruth loved thinking that orioles, with their vibrant livery, belonged to the lowly blackbird family. And her dear, elusive bluebirds, like robins, were first cousins of thrushes. When bluebirds still nested on the Kinneson farm, Ruth spent hours listening to the "whisper-song" of the male serenading his nesting mate.

Ruth stepped quickly off onto the gravel shoulder of the county road as a loaded logging truck roared past her. A brown thrasher flew low across the road from a shadblow thicket to a blackberry patch, directly in front of the oncoming 18-wheeler. There wasn't much left of the thrasher to lay gently under the shad copse, but though she was sorry for the bird, Ruth had lived in the country long enough to have developed an unsentimental view of death in the animal kingdom. Every year one or two brown thrashers got clipped along the county road between the red iron bridge and the village, where hedgerows crowded the macadam on both sides. Somewhere Ruth had read that thrashers had a repertoire of ten thousand distinct songs. Maybe she'd write about them, too. And definitely about meadowsweet.

At the cemetery on the east edge of the village Ruth made a short detour to visit the editor's grave. Carved into the granite marker above his name and dates and Ruth's name and birth date was a native brook trout about sixteen inches long. In 1760, when the editor's great-great-great-grandfather, Charles Kinneson I, had settled in what would become Kingdom County, he'd substituted a leaping brook trout for the Highlands stag rampant on the Kinneson family escutcheon. For two and a half

centuries the Vermont Kinnesons had been avid fly-fishers. At
first Ruth thought it was the fishing itself they loved, casting
the same vividly colored flies their Scottish ancestors had
favored, flies with names like Jock Scott, Royal Coachman,
Queen over the Water. In time Ruth realized that, even more
than the fishing, the Kinnesons loved the wild streams and
ponds where brook trout lived, and that, like their annual trip
to deer camp, fishing was most of all about family.

"Today's the day, sweetie," Ruth said.

*I thought so but I wasn't sure. After a while the days begin to
run together.*

"I just hope I'm doing the right thing."

*You always do the right thing. Say hello to your boyfriend for
me. Wish him luck.*

Ruth smiled. "You're my boyfriend. Besides, I'd have
thought you could wish him luck yourself. Then again, what
is it the Bible says? 'The dead know nothing.'"

*The Bible has it about half right, as usual. The dead know
some things. Not nothing. Sure as hell not everything.*

Still smiling, Ruth reached out and patted the brook trout
on the tombstone, half expecting the carved fish to dart away
from her hand. Family, she thought as she headed into the village. Fishing, hunting, baseball, the newspaper, the farm now
growing back to woods—all came down to family. In the Kingdom, family was everything.

*This building, the Kingdom Common Academy, was con-
structed over a ten-year period by the Reverend Dr. Pliny
Templeton. Using native pink or "Scotch" granite, and
working with a single team of Red Durham oxen, Dr. Tem-*

pleton began construction in 1857. He suspended work on the project from 1861 to 1865, when he served as Chaplain of the 2nd Vermont Regiment in the War of Southern Rebellion. He completed the school in 1867. During Dr. Templeton's tenure as headmaster, 1867–1900, more than 500 students graduated from the Academy. A former slave, and the first Negro to graduate from an American college, the beloved "Dr. T," as he was called by his students, bequeathed his skeleton to the Academy as an anatomical exhibit. In 1956, when the regional county high school opened, the Academy was sold to the Kingdom Common Library and Historical Society for a dollar. Dr. Templeton's skeleton may still be viewed during museum and library hours.

As many times as she'd read the plaque, Ruth was awed by the accomplishments of the Reverend Dr. Pliny Templeton. What the plaque did not say was even more important to her than what it did. It did not, for instance, disclose that Pliny's young bride, Lake Ponchartrain Templeton, had been sold down the river away from him on his twenty-first birthday. Nor did it state what everyone in the village had long known, that Ruth's husband's father, James Kinneson II, was Pliny's son by way of an out-of-wedlock liaison with the wild young daughter of Pliny's deliverer from slavery and adoptive brother, Charles "Mad Charlie" Kinneson II, who had gunned Pliny down in the church in their old age to prevent him from revealing James's true identity.

This morning Ruth had an early group of kids from a local day camp coming in for a tour, so after changing into her dress shoes, she went upstairs to open the museum. The historical exhibits were displayed in former classrooms according to theme, with each room dedicated to a different aspect of the county's history: Pre-mechanized farming. The Golden Age of Railroading. Lumbering and Log-driving in the Kingdom. Hunting and Fishing. And the Pliny Templeton Room, with Pliny's yellowing old skeleton, dressed in a somber black suit and wearing his clerical collar, dangling from a metal pole on the teacher's dais.

"Good morning, Dr. T," Ruth said, giving his handless left wrist a companionable fist bump.

Ruth looked out the tall windows of the former schoolroom at the village green below. A dozen or so Commoners were setting up open-air pavilions for the day ahead: Pliny Templeton Day. Their canvas tops glowed pastel pink and yellow and blue in the early-morning light. Later there would be a parade with floats depicting scenes from Pliny's life and times, and a chicken barbecue. A family-owned carnival out of southern New Hampshire had arrived the night before with an ancient merry-go-round and a few game and food booths. Also, there would be an old-fashioned baseball game between the Common and Kingdom Landing, using the same rules they'd used when Pliny introduced the game to the Kingdom after the Civil War.

"Happy birthday, Dr. T. Many happy returns."

"Forward-looking," Commoners said of Miss Ruth. She'd persuaded the library trustees to purchase computers and switch to a digital record-keeping system even before Jim computerized *The Monitor*. Ruth knew her way around the Internet before anyone else in the village, but kept the card catalogue, in its curly-maple cabinet, updated for older patrons. Also she was the first person in the Kingdom to go on Facebook and Twitter though she still wrote lively letters in her slightly shaky but elegant copperplate longhand.

Ruth loved to sit in the library office, formerly the Academy headmaster's, surrounded by her beloved books. Local school kids asked her if she had a favorite. Maybe *Pride and Prejudice*, she thought. Or *Romeo and Juliet*. Her deceased husband, the editor, said that there was never a well-told love story that Ruth didn't fall in love with. As long as it was a love story—*Cold Mountain, Brokeback Mountain, Lonesome Dove*—whatever story she was reading at the time was her favorite.

Promptly at eight o'clock, a gaggle of kids from the local day camp arrived for the first museum tour of the day. "Tell 'The Tale of the Viper's Abacus,' Miss Ruth," they clamored when she ushered them into the Pliny Templeton Room. "How Dr. T killed the great Louisiana diamondback when he was just a toddler."

"Well, guys, it was Pliny's granny who killed the diamondback. Pliny was about to step on a pretty vine twining over a log on the forest floor when 'JUMP, BOY!' Granny shouted. The vine, which was no vine at all, but a seven-foot-long rattlesnake, coiled and struck. Fortunately, it was still early in the morning and quite cool. The snake was sluggish. It missed Pliny's ankle but only by a little. Granny snatched it up by its buzzing tail. SNAP! She cracked that wicked old serpent in midair like a bullwhip, breaking its back instantly. The snake had twelve rattles on its tail. Granny cut it off and taught Pliny to count to ten on it, and the names of the twelve apostles. Later, he dyed the rattles in indigo and strung them on a thin silver chain for a necklace to give to his bride, Lake, as a wedding present. She wore them wherever she went. They said you could hear her coming because she ticked like a clock when she walked." At this point Ruth loved thinking to herself how the twelve indigo-colored rattles would have clicked together ecstatically when Lake and Pliny made love. Of course she never mentioned this to the school kids or tourists who visited the Athenaeum museum. Maybe parts of "The Tale of the Viper's Abacus" were apocryphal. That was fine. Ruth had never for a moment believed that a story needed to be factual to be true.

"Tell how Pliny lost his hand, Miss Ruth," Billy Quinn said. "How they sold his wife down the river and chained him by the wrist to a wrecked steamboat boiler and he cut off his hand at the wrist with a rusty old ax to free himself and search for his wife."

"I don't need to tell that story, Billy. You already have."

"He cut off his hand for freedom?" another boy asked.

"Not so much for freedom," said a little girl with snapping black eyes, Michelle Kittredge from Lost Nation Hollow. "For love."

"Exactly, sweetie," Ruth said. "Though the two go together, don't they? Freedom and love."

Michelle thought for a moment, then gave a solemn nod.

"Well, Miss Ruth, that is some tale," Arthur Showalter'd said back in May when Ruth finished her account. Arthur was a local attorney and president of the Athenaeum board. "But it doesn't change the fact that Pliny's skeleton belongs to the Athenaeum. As you know, in his will the Reverend Templeton donated his bones to the Kingdom Common Academy as an anatomical exhibit. When the Academy and Kingdom Landing were replaced by the central school, this building and all of its contents were sold to the library directors for a dollar."

"All that is very true, Arthur. However, there's the little matter of the Emancipation Proclamation. Not to mention the fact that the Kingdom Republic outlawed slavery in 1812."

"That's true, as well, Miss Ruth. But the Emancipation Proclamation applies to living human beings. Not to their earthly remains. Pliny—Dr. Templeton—is the museum's main draw. We can't just ship him back south on a sentimental whim. We don't even know if the woman in the mausoleum is his wife. Frankly, online family research outfits like the one you contacted are notorious for fabricating connections that never existed."

Ruth was amused. Even as a boy Artie Showalter had patronized his elders and contemporaries alike. "Where's King Solomon when we need him?" she told him now, smiling. "Knowing Old Sol, he might propose cutting Pliny's skeleton in half. We'll keep the top half and FedEx the bottom half to Baton Rouge. Or vice versa."

"That's hardly practicable, Miss Ruth."

"I was just injecting a little levity into the conversation, Arthur. You know. Being facetious."

Then Ruth had made one more attempt to explain. Above all she didn't want it said later that she hadn't given the trustees every opportunity to do the right thing. "Pliny and Lake should never again belong to anyone but each other. Two quick questions. Is there anyone in this room who's never been in love?"

No hands went up.

"Question number two: Is there anyone here who doubts what Pliny's choice in this matter would be?"

Again, no one, though the board voted 7–2 to keep Pliny's skeleton. "I'm sorry, Miss Ruth," George Quinn Jr. said. "On the bottom line, it's a question of property ownership."

Ruth sighed. "It always has been, hasn't it," she said. It wasn't a question.

Unbidden, as if of their own accord, Ruth's Pliny stories spooled out over the course of the morning as visitors toured the museum. How Pliny won his wife, Lake, in a race around a molasses barrel against a Kentucky quarter horse, Pliny's father and master having staked him against the horse and Lake. How, after chopping off his hand to free himself, he'd fled *south*, rather than north, in search of his wife. Come north with the help of Charles Kinneson II, gone on the abolition speaking circuit, worked his way through the state university and Princeton Theological Seminary, and much, much more.

"Did he ever find his wife?" Sooner or later someone would always ask this question. Sometimes a man, more often a woman.

And Ruth always replied, "Not yet."

She ended her tours by explaining that sometimes Pliny the man and Pliny the myth blended together. Did he really wrestle alligators? Tackle his deliverer and adoptive brother, Mad Charlie

Kinneson, to prevent him from mounting a one-man counter-charge at Gettysburg? Did his skeleton, as legend had it, occasionally reach up and detach itself from its pole to go ghosting through the village late at night searching for his long-lost wife?

"I don't really believe in ghosts, do you?" Ruth asked the kids.

"Nooo, Miss Ruth," they'd chorus, all the more sure now that the rumors of the walking skeleton were true. It was her "really" that hooked them. "I don't *really* believe in ghosts."

But it was the unsolved story of the star-crossed lovers, separated like Longfellow's Gabriel and Evangeline, that visitors to the museum liked best. Not unrequited. Not unconsummated. Unresolved.

At noon Ruth ate a cup of yogurt, and a lettuce sandwich, her own homegrown lettuce on her own homemade bread. She'd closed the museum and library until three o'clock so she could see the parade and the reenactment of the first baseball game, in 1868, between the Common and the Landing. She decided to watch the ball game with Pliny from his room on the second floor of the Athenaeum.

When Ruth had first come to Kingdom County as a young bride herself, no older than Pliny and Lake when they'd first gotten married, she'd known nothing at all about baseball, except that it seemed the most interminable and tedious game in the history of the world. By degrees, watching her husband the editor play the game, and his father, James Kinneson II, who pitched for the Kingdom County Outlaws into his sixties, then her sons, then her grandsons, she'd become first an aficionado, then something of an expert on its endless and sometimes nearly maddening intricacies.

The three-inning game between the Common and the Landing featured Judge Charlie as Pliny, in an old-fashioned uniform resembling nothing so much as a striped convict's suit, pitching underhanded from just forty feet away from the batter. Gloveless fielders pegged the ball directly at the baserunners to get them out. The Landing won 46–12, the game ending with a staged brawl between the two teams and their fans, in which "Pliny" pretended once again to shatter the jaw of Prof. Cedric Benson, the Landing's headmaster. Charlie's teammates hoisted him to their shoulders and carried him around the bases singing "For He's a Jolly Good Fellow."

After the game and the rhubarb came the parade around the Common, led by the remnants of the town band. Once upward of forty uniformed musicians had serenaded the village from the bandstand each Saturday evening throughout the summer. The band had dwindled to a dozen elderly stalwarts blaring out "When Johnny Comes Marching Home" and, unaccountably, "Dixie." And here came the floats on antique farm trucks and hay wagons pulled by vintage tractors. Each tableau depicted a different event from Pliny's life and times. Pliny arm-wrestling John Brown, driving Brown right out of his chair onto the puncheon floor of his cabin at Pliny's interview to go on the circuit. Brown rising sheepishly and saying, "You'll do." Pliny in his clerical robes, descanting from the pulpit. Pliny wielding his schoolmastering cane, Jack Regulator, and sitting at his desk working on his great history of the Kingdom. It was all very inspiring and entertaining but also,

Ruth thought, vaguely disingenuous. As if, in the end, the parade was more about the Kingdom and Pliny Templeton Day than about Pliny himself. And where was the tableau of Mad Charlie Kinneson gunning down Pliny in his own church, on Easter morning, because Pliny wanted his beloved son, James II, to know who he truly was? Might Pliny be thinking the same thing? Ruth didn't know.

Through the open windows of the former science room of the Academy Ruth could smell the barbecue grilling behind the church. She would buy a supper box: half a chicken (a breast and a thigh), a baked potato, salad, a roll, coffee.

"I suppose I have to go down there and show my face," Ruth told the old schoolmaster. "After my little setback with the trustees a few weeks ago. Whenever my husband lost a cause he'd been editorializing for, he'd make it a point to show his face everywhere in the village. Drop by the hotel dining room for coffee. Stick his head in the post office, say hello to the drugstore cowboys. Shake hands with his opponents and congratulate them in *The Monitor*. Maybe play catch with Charlie or Jimmy on the common. I've got to go kill the trustees with kindness."

Before sitting down to eat in the Harmony Room of the church, Ruth made a point of circulating from table to table to congratulate the elders on the success of Pliny Templeton Day. She ate with Jim and Frannie and Charlie and Athena, then took a turn down the midway of the carnival on the village green. The colored lights on the game booths and rides glowed in the twilight. Years ago a shabby circus had come to the Common for a one-night stand. In the "Wonders of the Seven Continents" sideshow, a snake charmer had displayed a four-foot-long boa, a docile and somnolent animal named Monty, which allowed its handler to make of it like a puppy. Somehow the creature had gotten loose from its cage that night. An intense, village-wide search ensued to no avail. The circus had to leave for its next engagement without Monty. Several days later Ruth glanced out of the window of her office to see a gathering around the jungle gym in the playground of the former Academy. She knew immediately that the missing constrictor had turned up. The snake had wound its way into the upper bars of the jungle gym to catch the warm early sun. Ruth arrived just as Harlan Kittredge roared into the parking lot in his pickup, flying the Confederate flag from its aerial, the gun rack bristling with Harlan's 12-gauge Ithaca and Browning semiautomatic. "We won't need to exercise our Second Amendment rights this morning, Harlan," Ruth had famously said. She reached up and lifted the reptile off its perch and carried it into the Athenaeum to what would become its new home—a spacious terrarium left behind years ago when the villages of Kingdom Common and Kingdom Landing joined together to build a union school midway between the two towns. Stories, Ruth thought. So many stories. In the end, stories and love were what you were left with.

Ruth had left the light on over the loading dock behind the school but still was surprised to find the SUV with out-of-state plates parked there, the driver waiting beside it. She was much younger than Ruth had expected, not yet thirty, and she had dark eyes and hair. She was tall and slender, and wore designer jeans and expensive hiking boots and a denim shirt. The sort of outfit a city person on vacation in the country might wear. She was beautiful. There was a spectral aura about the way she and the SUV had materialized and, it occurred to Ruth, probably about herself as well, standing under the dock light in her white dress like a revenant.

"Madame Kinneson?" the girl—Ruth could not help seeing her as a girl—said. "Madame Ruth Kinneson?"

"Professor Ducharmes?" Ruth extended her hand as the young woman came up the concrete steps of the dock. "How do you do? Yes, I'm Ruth Kinneson—the mischief maker who started all of this foolishness."

The young woman—how could she possibly be old enough to be a professor?—and Ruth shook hands. Then the girl threw her arms around Ruth and hugged her closely. "Madame Kinneson," she said. "My unindicted co-conspirator."

Professor Ducharmes laughed as though she and Ruth had known each other forever and were now about to embark on one last great adventure together. Then both women were laughing, hugging each other and laughing like schoolgirls.

"Thank you, Professor, for coming all this way to indulge an old woman."

"Not 'Professor,' Madame Kinneson. Lake."

"Not 'Madame Kinneson,' Lake. Ruth," Ruth said. Like Dr. Frannie, Lake Ducharmes had a slight French accent—Cajun in her case, of course—and she was clearly delighted to be in Kingdom County. Ruth noticed that she was wearing an engagement ring.

"Well, dear, let's go meet your great-great-great-grandfather."

On their way upstairs Lake said, "So this is my ancestor's great stone school. He, too, like me, was a teacher. I imagine he was a tartar. Was he a tartar, Miss Ruth?"

"His students called him 'Old Dr. Bluster.' His bark was worse than his bite."

"Your Athenaeum, Miss Ruth. It still smells like a school. You must know that my family, from my original namesake on down, was overflowing with teachers. For us, I mean for the women of the family, schoolteaching was the pathway to some social equality. Not to be inquisitive, Miss Ruth, did you teach?"

Ruth laughed. "No, Lake. I raised two boys. Believe me, that was a full-time job."

"Boys are an exceedingly troublesome species. I know, I have four brothers. Also—I saw you glance at my ring—a fiancé in Baton Rouge who is insanely overprotective. He did not wish for me to make this trip into the land of northern aggression alone. I told him that the matter was between me and my ancestor. That Pliny stole himself once before by cutting off his hand to search for his wife, my great-great-great-grandmother Lake, and I now intended to help him steal himself again. If you don't mind me asking, Miss Ruth, how did the meeting with your board of directors go?"

Ruth paused on the landing midway up the stairs. "About the way I expected, dear. They listened politely. Then they voted not to let Pliny go."

" 'Way down in Egypt Land,' " Lake sang. " 'Let my people go.' Nothing changes, does it, Miss Ruth? How surprised your trustees will be to discover that the old boy has flown the coop."

Ruth was beginning to realize that her distant in-law was amused by everything they were doing. She reminded Ruth of her daughters-in-law, Athena and Frannie. They stepped inside the Pliny Templeton Room but Ruth did not turn on the lights. They could see what they needed to by the street lights outside the windows and the lighted rides on the green.

"Professor Ducharmes, I'd like you to meet the Reverend Dr. Pliny Templeton. Dr. T, I'm honored to introduce you to your and Lake's great-great-great-granddaughter, Lake Ponchartrain Ducharmes."

Lake reached out and touched Pliny's wrist where his hand should be. "So it's true. He cut off his own hand to search for his wife. Well, before my own fiancé sends out the marines after me, shall we get on with it?"

Ruth nodded at Pliny's pole. "If you'll do the honors, Lake, I'll get the doors. Don't worry. He won't fall apart. He's well-knit."

With Ruth going ahead and Lake following, carrying Pliny on his pole, still laughing, the unindicted co-conspirators made their way downstairs, through the library and out onto the landing dock.

"Let's put him up front," Lake said. "Let him ride shotgun and enjoy the sights."

Still laughing, they belted the headmaster in, with the pole on the floor in back. From the Common came the faint strains of the carousel music: "I'm off to join the circus."

Lake opened the glove compartment and removed a flat, narrow, rectangular box about as long as her hand, wrapped in light-blue gift paper. "Put this in your purse, Miss Ruth. Open it at home, *s'il vous plaît*."

Then Lake embraced Ruth again and went away in the SUV with Pliny propped up in the seat beside her, down the gravel service road behind the school, past the long-abandoned American Heritage furniture factory, and south on I-91 toward Pliny's final resting place. The last Ruth glimpsed of her, she seemed to be talking to her ancestor.

"He's on his way," Ruth told the editor ten minutes later. "You'd like the girl. She is, as they say, a pistol. I hope this was the right thing to do."

It was the only thing to do.

Ruth patted their stone, still warm to the touch from the heat of the day. In the moonlight, she could make out their names carved into the granite. "See you soon, sweetie."

Ruth had already taken three or four steps before she remembered. She returned to the tombstone, removed from her purse the flat box Lake had given her and unwrapped it. Inside, on a layer of tissue, lay a necklace. A necklace with twelve indigo-blue stones on a thin silver chain. Ruth poured it out into her hand. There in her palm, shimmering in the moonlight, lay the viper's abacus, passed down to Lake Ponchartrain Ducharmes, and on to Ruth, through five generations of Louisiana women. Weightless as love.

Charlie and Athena had stopped in with leftover birthday cake from the celebration on the Common. BIRT Ruth's slice announced in pink frosting. Jim and Frannie joined them at the kitchen table in Ruth's side of the farmhouse. She showed them the necklace and wondered aloud if it should be returned to Lake Ponchartrain Templeton.

"She's got Pliny," Charlie said. "or soon will have. She doesn't need a necklace made from a snake's tail."

And a few minutes later, after Charlie and Athena had gone home, as Ruth sipped a good-night cup of coffee at the table, she heard Frannie say through the stovepipe hole, "Well, James, love conquers all."

"I'm positive of it," Jimmy said. "I'm just not sure it can be proven."

"Of course it can be," Frannie said. "Where's Mom? Did she go up to bed?"

"I think so. How can you prove it?"

Ruth smiled to herself. She suspected where this conversation was headed, she'd heard it before.

"Come upstairs with me, James. I'll prove it to you right now."

Ruth had just enough strength left to wash up, brush her teeth, and get ready for bed herself. She was amused by the events of the day, by her conversations with the long-gone and not so long-gone dead, by Frannie and Jim's concern for her delicate ears, and by the impossibility of making anything of anything but love.

Then she heard, quite distinctly:

It took you long enough to get here, boy.

I searched high and low.

Come on in where it cool. Member that race you and Lady Ebony run? How you won me?

I remember the first time I saw you. Balancing the full glass of water on your head. Smiling across the ballroom at me.

I never! Jez'bel all over again! Come Mardi Gras, we'll go dancing, I and you. Down Bourbon Street. Oh, yeah.

In the morning Ruth would write her column for *The Monitor*. Something about the songbirds of Vermont. How while the female bluebird sat on her eggs, the male whistled to her softly. She could hear him whistling as she drifted off to sleep. Up in Kingdom County, in the far northern mountains of Vermont, Pliny Templeton Day was over.